THE PROUD PRINCESS

Ilona knew what it meant to be alone. Knew how it felt to be hungry, mistreated, defenseless.

But now Ilona was going home. All the hardships of exile were behind her. She was going back to Dabrozka, the tiny kingdom whose throne would someday be hers. She was returning triumphant —the beloved Princess of a proud and independent people who needed her desperately.

Ilona was Dabrozka's last hope for salvation. She alone could save her subjects from domination if she married a man who despised her. A man with whom Ilona was already falling wildly in love.

BARBARA CARTLAND

Bantam Books by Barbara Cartland
Ask your bookseller for the books you have missed

Barbara Cartland
The Proud Princess

THE PROUD PRINCESS
A Bantam Book | November 1976

ISBN 0-553-02958-4

Published simultaneously in the United States and Canada

Bantam Books are published by Bantam Books, Inc. Its trade-
mark, consisting of the words "Bantam Books" and the por-
trayal of a bantam, is registered in the United States Patent
Office and in other countries. Marca Registrada. Bantam
Books, Inc., 666 Fifth Avenue, New York, New York 10019.

Chapter One

1872

Ilona glanced back over her shoulder as she galloped wildly through the trees.

They thinned out until she saw the broad open steppe with its brilliant green grass richly interspersed with flowers.

It was very beautiful, fading away to an indeterminate horizon beneath the wooded slopes that rose higher and higher until they touched the snow-peaked mountains.

But Ilona realised that once she was in the open country she would be in full view of those who were following her.

"Could anything," she asked herself, "be more frustrating than to go riding accompanied by two elderly Army officers and two grooms?"

She had looked incredulously at her escort when she walked down the steps of the Palace!

Then as they set off, moving at what she thought of as an almost funereal pace, she knew she had no intention of riding for long in such a pompous manner.

The one thing she had looked forward to on her journey home was the horses.

She had been only ten when she left Dabrozka, but she had never forgotten the thrill of riding over its grassy steppes and the unique magnificence of its fiery steeds.

Bred on the equivalent of the great Hortobágy Puszia, which was the most famous and largest of its kind

1

in Hungary, the Dabrozkan horses were reared in the same utter wildness as the Hungarian colts, which were world-famous.

In fact, like the people, the horses of Dabrozka had more Hungarian blood in them than those of any other country in the Balkans.

Magyar, Roman, Hungarian, and Greek, all were in the blood and in the age-old history of the Dabrozkans, but Ilona preferred to remember only their Greek and Hungarian ancestry.

She felt that these contributed more to her looks, character, and personality than did any of the others.

It was the Hungarian in her now that made her determined to escape and enjoy the freedom of the wind on her cheeks and the enchanting beauty of her surroundings.

She realised, as she guided her horse through almost the last of the trees, that on her left lay the river that divided the valley like a silver ribbon.

On an impulse she turned her horse's head and descended the steep bank, aware that she was moving too fast for safety, but being certain that the Dabrozkan animal was sure-footed enough not to throw her.

Reaching the edge of the river, she glanced back and saw that there was as yet no sign of her four chaperons following her through the trees.

As she had expected at this time of year, the river was low and in another month would be no more than a shallow stream.

It was at the moment flowing silver over its stony bed, but the water was clear and it was easy to see the bottom.

Giving her horse just a touch of the whip, to which he responded immediately, Ilona guided him into the river and found she was right in her assumption that it was not too deep for them to cross. In fact the water did not reach her stirrup.

They climbed out the other side and disappeared into the thickness of the pine-woods while there was still no chance of being seen.

Ilona bent forward to pat her horse's neck.

"We have done it, boy," she said in her soft voice, "and now we can enjoy ourselves!"

She could not help thinking as she spoke that her father would be very annoyed, but just for once she was not afraid of him.

He would take her to task, there was no doubt about that, if the men escorting her were unwise enough to report that they had failed in their duty.

Ilona had the idea that when it came to the point, as long as they could bring her back to the Palace intact, they were unlikely to court trouble.

The pine-trees smelt delicious in the warmth of the sun, and since there was now no hurry she proceeded through them, looking about her.

She was hoping for a sight of the wild animals which had fascinated her as a child.

In Dabrozka there were chamois, bear, wolf, lynx, stag, and wild boar.

She would never forget the tiny baby bear-cubs that had been brought for her inspection when she was a little girl, and which the gypsies tamed and took with them to the Fairs in the countryside.

She had learnt that it was impossible to tame or teach an old bear, but the cubs, if they were taken from their mother early enough, were very amenable and were seldom savage as they were in their wild state.

There was however no sign of any bears in this forest, but only a profusion of birds, which flew away at her approach, some of them protesting volubly at her intrusion.

The shafts of sunshine coming through the branches of the pine-trees seemed to give the place a magic which Ilona had never forgotten.

It was all part of the legends and fairy-stories of her childhood.

She remembered now how she had always believed there were dragons living in the depths of the pine-woods, goblins burrowing under the hills, and mystic, ethereal beings like the Greek gods living amongst the snow-covered peaks.

Ilona was humming a little tune to herself, a peasant song which came from the past, when suddenly she heard voices.

Instinctively she reined in her horse and listened.

There were a number of people speaking and she thought that was strange, because usually there was no-one in the woods at this time of the day.

The peasants would be in the fields, cultivating the fertile acres, under the strict supervision of an overseer.

Then she thought that perhaps it was the woodcutters she heard.

She tried to remember if this was the time of year when the trees were felled and the great logs were carried down the valley by the river.

But she told herself there was not enough water in the river to float logs, and anyway there seemed to be too many voices for wood-cutters.

Because she was curious she moved in the direction of the sound.

Twisting in and out of the pine-trees, her horse's hooves made very little sound on the soft moss and sand beneath them.

Then unexpectedly she could see through the trees a large clearing and in it were a number of men, perhaps fifty or more.

Ilona looked at them with interest.

They were wearing white baggy trousers and embroidered white coats which hung Huzzar fashion from one shoulder.

On their heads they wore black round felt hats sporting a single large feather, which gave them a dashing air that was characteristic of the Dabrozkans.

Ilona looked to see if there were any women in the gathering, but they were all men. Strangely enough, they did not look like the poorest peasant labourers that she might have expected to find in the wood.

She was so intent on what she was seeing that without her realising it her horse had moved on through the trees, and now she was in sight of the men in the clearing.

They were all talking very quickly and passionately, gesticulating with their arms, and as far as Ilona could understand they were proclaiming violently against something or somebody.

She realised as she listened that the years she had been away had made it difficult for her to understand the peasants' language as she had been able to do before she left home.

With her mother she had always talked in Hungarian or French, but Dabrozkan was a language of many inflections and many different accents.

The ordinary people spoke a mixed language derived from the countries that bordered their own.

Besides Hungarian, there were many words that were Romanian or Russian.

But Ilona was sure of two words that she heard. One was "fight" and the other was "injustice."

Then a man who was speaking furiously and undoubtedly sincerely, declaiming almost like an orator, saw Ilona.

The words appeared to die on his lips and she thought there was a ludicrous expression on his face as he stared at her, suddenly speechless.

The majority of the other men had their backs to her and now they turned round and stared too.

There was a silence that seemed all the more impressive because of the noise they had been making.

Then the man who had been speaking pointed at Ilona and shouted:

"Who is she? What does she want? We have been betrayed!"

There was a sudden murmur from the men sitting on the ground on felled logs, and they rose to their feet.

For the first time Ilona felt a tremor of fear.

Apart from rising to their feet, they had not moved towards her. Yet she had the impression of danger, of something she did not understand, and it was menacing.

From the far end of the crowd a man who had not risen with the others now got to his feet.

He walked towards her and she saw he was very tall and that he gave the impression of being better dressed than the rest.

He reached her side and she saw that he was in fact extremely good-looking, with the straight, almost classical features that she had always attributed to the Dabrozkans' Greek antecedents.

But surprisingly, though his hair was very dark, his eyes were vividly blue.

There were Hungarians with that particular colouring, and occasionally it appeared amongst the Dabrozkans; but Ilona had never seen a man look quite so arresting or so attractive.

"What do you want?" he asked.

She realised as he spoke that his voice was cultured and he was speaking in the pure, upper-class Dabrozkan language that was almost Hungarian.

"As you can see," she replied. "I am riding."

She thought there was a faint smile on his lips as he replied:

"I am aware of that. You are not wise to be in this part of the wood."

"Why not?" Ilona asked in astonishment.

As her father's daughter she knew she could ride anywhere she wished in Dabrozka, and no land, whoever it belonged to, could be closed to the King or his family.

"Are you alone?" the man asked.

"I should have thought any answer to that question was quite unnecessary," Ilona retorted.

She came to the conclusion that he was being impertinent.

He might not realise who she was, but at the same time there was a note in his voice that she resented, and he asked his questions in an authoritative manner, to which she was sure he had no right.

He glanced down at her horse's legs and saw that they were wet.

"You have crossed the river!" he said, and it was an accusation. "Let me suggest, young woman, that you return the way you came."

6

"I will return when I am ready to do so, and not a moment before!"

Ilona did not know why she felt so truculent.

Ordinarily she would have been perfectly amenable and willing to do anything that anyone asked of her; but now she felt defiant and her chin went up as she said:

"I cannot imagine what is going on here, unless you are taking part in some secret and subversive activity of which you are ashamed."

She spoke clearly, and the men on the outskirts of the crowd who were nearest to her must have understood what she had said.

There was a sudden movement and they started to speak in low voices to one another.

The man with the blue eyes put his hand on the bridle of her horse and started to lead her back into the wood through which she had come.

"Kindly take your hand off my bridle!" Ilona ordered.

"Do not be a little fool!" the man answered contemptuously. "If you know what is good for you, you will go away and forget anything you may have seen or heard."

"And why should I do that?"

"Because, as I have already said," he answered, "it would be dangerous for you to do otherwise."

"Dangerous? Dangerous for whom?"

He did not answer but went on leading her horse between the trees.

Ilona pulled the bridle sharply so that the horse came to a standstill.

"I do not like your attitude!" she said. "I will not be ordered about by you or anyone else!"

The man looked at her for a moment, then said:

"Now listen to me, and listen carefully."

There was something in the tone of his voice that made the words that were on Ilona's lips die away.

She looked down at him and was still.

"I do not know who you are or why you should come here," he said. "Presumably you are a visitor to

7

this country. But let me beg you, for your own sake and everyone else's, to go away quickly. Forget what you have seen!"

"What have I seen?" Ilona asked. "A lot of men gathered together in the centre of a wood talking of injustice."

"So you heard that, did you?"

"I heard it," Ilona replied. "But I am prepared to forget it if you will give me a good reason why I should do so."

"I thought I had given you one already," he answered, "but if you want to do a great deal of harm, perhaps unintentionally, if you want to destroy men who are important to Dabrozka, then chatter about what you have seen and heard."

There was a note of sincerity in his voice that had not been there before.

Because she had the feeling that he was telling the truth and that it was important, Ilona capitulated.

"Very well," she said quietly. "You have my word that I will not tell anyone that I have been here."

She thought she saw an expression of relief in his eyes.

At the same time, because she thought he was likely to be too pleased with himself for having got his own way, she added:

"Nevertheless, I see no reason why you should be so intolerably bossy and order me about."

For the first time the man smiled. It undoubtedly made him appear even more attractive than he had before.

"How would you like me to be?" he enquired. "Humble and conciliatory?"

He was mocking her and there was a little spark of resentment in Ilona's eyes.

Then astonishingly, before she was aware of his intentions, he put out his arms and lifted her from the saddle.

Before she could fight against him, before she actually had the slightest idea of what he was about to do, his lips came down on hers and he kissed her!

She was so astonished that she was stunned into immobility as his mouth held hers captive and his arms encircled her.

Then as swiftly as he had lifted her down he put her back in the saddle.

As her hands instinctively went out to the reins to steady herself, he said:

"You are far too lovely to be concerned with politics! Go home, pretty lady, and flirt with your beaux!"

She stared at him, for the moment speechless, unable to collect her senses or realise what had happened.

Then as he finished speaking he slapped her horse hard on the behind and as the animal jerked forward Ilona saw the river just ahead of her.

She reached the water and the horse was wading through the river before she realised what was happening.

"How dare he . . . how dare he kiss me?"

It was incredible! Unbelievable! An outrage!

And yet, she thought helplessly, she had done nothing about it!

She should have screamed, hit him with her whip, or at least fought him furiously and frantically, as any respectable girl would have done.

But in actual fact she had done nothing!

She had just let him hold her in his arms and kiss her lips.

Ilona had never been kissed before.

In fact no-one had ever attempted it, and she had not realised that a man's mouth could hold one completely captive or that his lips would be so firm, hard, and demanding.

She had always imagined that a kiss would be something very soft and gentle, but this stranger's kiss seemed to violate her in a manner that she could not explain even to herself.

It was as if he possessed her and she had been subservient to him.

She felt her cheeks burn at the thought.

She was so intent on her own thoughts that she did

not realise until she reached the other side of the river that standing on the bank waiting for her was her escort.

The Army officers and the grooms were looking, she thought, exceedingly disapproving! As well they might, if they knew what had happened!

"Thank goodness Your Royal Highness is safe!" Colonel Ceáky ejaculated. "But you should not have crossed the river!"

"Why not?" Ilona questioned.

"We realise, Princess, that your horse bolted with you," the Colonel said slowly, as if choosing his words with care, "but it was very unfortunate, Your Royal Highness, that you should have been carried into Sáros territory."

"Apparently no harm has been done," the other officer remarked.

"No, of course," the Colonel agreed. "At the same time, Princess, we must beg you to be more careful another time."

Ilona turned her horse towards the open steppe in front of them.

She was well aware that the Colonel, in speaking of her horse having bolted, had found an excuse for their own incompetence in letting her escape them.

But she was not concerned with that.

What interested her was the serious note in his voice when he said that she should not enter Sáros territory.

"As you know, Colonel," she said aloud, "I have not been in Dabrozka since I was ten years old. I cannot remember there being any restrictions in those days about crossing the river. Of course, I may have forgotten."

She was aware that Colonel Ceáky glanced at the Major as if in doubt of what they should tell her.

There was also an expression almost of fear in his eyes, but that, she thought, could be accounted for by the fact that they were afraid of her father.

Who was not?

Even in the twenty-four hours she had been at home she had realised that everyone in the Palace almost grovelled before him and watched him apprehensively.

"Why did I not stay in Paris?" she asked herself.

Then she remembered that she had had no choice in the matter.

"I would like to know the truth," she said to the Colonel. "What are you suggesting by saying that I should not enter Sáros territory?"

She paused and added with a faint smile on her lips:

"Whatever you tell me, I will not repeat it to the King."

She was almost certain that the Colonel relaxed a little as he answered:

"Our country, although Your Royal Highness may not be aware of it, is divided into two sections. Radák and Sáros."

"But surely Papa reigns over the whole of Dabrozka, as my grandfather did and his father before him?"

"In theory," the Colonel replied, "but in the last five or six years things have altered dramatically."

"In what way?" Ilona asked.

She was very interested, and although they were now on the flat grassland of the steppes she made no effort to gallop her horse as ordinarily she would have done.

The two grooms were some way behind them and she realised that if they kept their voices low she and the two officers could not be overheard.

"Please go on!" she begged.

"The Princes of Sáros have always been the largest and most powerful landowners in Dabrozka," the Colonel said, "and in your grandfather's time the head of the family, Prince Ladislas, was next to the King, the most important man in the country."

"One might almost say they shared their power," Major Kassa interposed.

"Yes, that is right! The two men together administered the country most ably," the Colonel agreed.

There was a pause, then he said:

"It was very different when your father, Prince Jozef Radák, inherited the Throne."

11

There was no need for Ilona to ask why.

Her father's irascible temper, his overbearing character, and his cruelty had driven her mother from Dabrozka, and she herself had hated him ever since she was old enough to think.

"What is happening now?" she asked.

"Dabrozka really consists of two separate States," the Colonel explained, "and the people live either in Radák land or in Sáros."

"There is almost a state of war between the two sections," Major Kassa explained.

"A state of war?" Ilona exclaimed.

She had hoped when she left France that she need never think of war again, and yet it was apparently to be found even in Dabrozka.

"Dabrozkans are in a very difficult position," the Colonel explained. "Because their Rulers are at enmity, some citizens find it an excuse to pay off old grudges, to renew feuds, and to revenge ancient insults."

"You mean," Ilona said, "that the Sáros section is fighting us?"

There was a pause. Then the Colonel said tentatively:

"Prince Aladár Sáros disapproves and rejects many of the new laws that have been introduced by His Majesty. He refuses to obey them and defends his people when they are arrested."

"Does he defend them by force?" Ilona asked.

"Two nights ago," the Colonel replied, "the prison in Vitózi was broken into and all the prisoners were released!"

"Were the soldiers who were guarding them . . . killed?"

"None of them," the Colonel replied. "They were all bound and thrown into the lake! It was not deep enough for them to drown, but it was a humiliation they will not forget in a hurry."

The Colonel's voice was grim.

Ilona laughed. She could not help it.

"It is not a matter for amusement, Your Royal Highness," Major Kassa said reprovingly.

"I am sorry," Ilona apologised, "but I was thinking only yesterday when I watched the guard at the Palace how pompous the soldiers looked in the new uniform Papa has chosen for them! To see them bound and sitting in the lake must have been amusing for the citizens of Vitózi, while the victims resented the indignity of it!"

"I am only trying to warn Your Royal Highness," Colonel Ceáky said with a reproachful note in his voice, "that you should not go into Sáros territory. You might be insulted, or worse still, I would not be surprised if you were kidnapped!"

He paused before he said impressively:

"It would certainly be a way to induce His Majesty to rescind some of his new laws."

"What are these new laws that have caused so much trouble?" Ilona asked.

The Colonel looked uncomfortable.

"I think perhaps you should ask the King that question, Your Royal Highness."

"You know perfectly well that I would not wish to do that," Ilona replied. "I am just as frightened of Papa as you are, Colonel."

"Frightened? Frightened?" the Colonel ejaculated. "I have a vast respect for His Majesty, and I obey his commands."

"But you are frightened of him," Ilona insisted. "Come on, be honest and own up! Papa is a very frightening person. That is why for me it has been such a relief however difficult it has been, not to live in Dabrozka all these years."

She gave a little sigh and looked round her.

"At the same time, I have missed its incredible beauty and of course our wonderful, wonderful horses!"

She bent forward to pat her mount. Then when she would have ridden on she sat up again and said resolutely:

"Tell me the truth, Colonel, and then we will gallop over this glorious ground."

The Colonel looked at her and she thought his eyes softened, as if he found the appeal in hers irresistible.

"Very well then," he replied. "I will tell you, Princess, that the two laws that have most infuriated a great number of people are, first—the King has decreed that half of every man's harvest shall be appropriated by the State!"

"In other words . . . by him!" Ilona said in a low voice.

"Secondly," the Colonel went on as if he had not been interrupted, "he has banished all gypsies under pain of death."

"But that is ridiculous!" Ilona exclaimed. "The gypsies have always lived peacefully with us. I remember Mama telling me how cruelly they were treated in Romania and all the terrible tortures to which they were subjected."

She paused before she went on reflectively:

"In Hungary too there is a long history of persecutions and torture under Maria Thérèsa and then Joseph II."

"That is true, Princess," Major Kassa murmured.

"But here they have always been accepted as part of our way of life," Ilona said.

"The King has said that they are to leave the country," Colonel Ceáky remarked.

"But where will they go?" Ilona asked. "There is only Russia, and as the Russians dislike us so much it is unlikely that they will accept our gypsies."

"These arguments have all been put to the King, and very forcibly indeed, by Prince Aladár."

"You need not tell me that he would not listen," Ilona murmured.

"There are a number of other laws that have recently been proclaimed and which are causing much dissention," the Colonel said. "The Army is being reinforced, but the situation, I can say quite frankly, is not a comfortable one."

"I am not surprised!"

Ilona smiled at the Colonel, then at the Major.

"Thank you, gentlemen, for what you have told me. You may rest assured that I will not betray your confidence."

She looked ahead as she said:

"Now I want to gallop as swiftly as I can and forget everything except that this is the most beautiful place in the world!"

She touched her horse with her whip and he sprang forward as if as eager as she was to gallop over the grassy steppe.

As the horses thundered over the soft ground, Ilona thought it was the most marvellous sensation she had ever known.

Riding homewards, she could not help looking at the peasants they passed working in the fields, busy in the small villages or in the woods that surrounded the Palace.

Was it her imagination, she asked herself, or did they look sulky and resentful?

Or had she been wrong in remembering a smiling, good-tempered people who had been her countrymen in the past?

The wooden houses with their balconies filled with flowers, and the *Csardas,* or wayside Inns, with their painted signs and vine-covered gardens where the customers congregated to drink the local wine, were just as she remembered them.

The acacia-trees were in bloom and the whole scene looked not only beautiful but prosperous.

The large herds of cows, their white horns polished and often decorated with ribbons, and the flocks of fleecy sheep and black and white foals were unchanged.

Many of the women, with brightly coloured skirts and long plaits of hair reaching nearly to their knees, were very beautiful.

The men all had a picturesque raffishness about them.

It was due, Ilona thought, to their Hussar-type jackets, carelessly flung over one shoulder, their red waistcoats plenteously ornamented with buttons, and their round, felt hats with their cheeky feathers.

Some wore top-boots with spurs but rode their horses bare-backed, and Ilona knew that their horsemanship could not be equalled by the men of any country in Europe.

Everything seemed as it had always been, and yet she told herself there was something lacking! Then she realised what it was.

Always she had associated music, singing, and laughter with the Dabrozkans.

They used to sing as they worked, as they drove their cattle out to pasture, and when they came home triumphantly from a hunting expedition, carrying a chamois or a stag tied to a pole that rested on their shoulders.

But now, she noticed, there seemed to be a silence over the land, and she was sure too that the peasants' clothes were more shabby and threadbare than they had been in the past.

The gypsies had often been in tatters, but not the peasants, who had always taken a very personal pride in their appearance.

They neared the Palace and started the long climb up to the magnificent building, which had stood high above the valley for centuries.

It had been built and rebuilt by every succeeding Monarch.

But Ilona's grandfather had made it even more impressive and impregnable by adding more towers and turrets to the existing building.

From a distance the Palace looked a most beautiful building.

But near it was a grim reminder of the days when to defend a fortress it was always wisest to be above the enemy, and to be able to shoot him down as he approached.

Ilona's grandmother had planted trees all round the Castle to make it, she had said, look less awe-inspiring.

When the almond-blossom and peach-trees were in bloom, its towers and spires seemed to rise like an insubstantial dream from the exquisite pink-and-white blossoms.

The gardens inside the Castle were also very lovely.

As she entered through the great iron gate that had repelled enemy Armies and marauding bands, Ilona thought that no-one living in such beautiful surroundings should be anything but happy.

But as she knew only too well, there was no happiness inside the Radák Palace.

She had thought never to see her home again. In fact, her mother had said to her often enough:

"We will never go back, Ilona. We may not be important abroad, we may have little money, but at least we have peace of mind."

When she spoke of the past, Ilona's mother always had an expression of horror in her eyes and a note of fear in her voice that was very disturbing.

At first Ilona had not understood why her mother was prepared to give up her position as Queen in Dabrozka, to leave her friends and the life she had known for eighteen years.

When the Queen Gisela had left her husband, she had done it very quietly in an undramatic manner that in itself was more impressive than if she had made a scene or invited sympathy.

She had suffered at the hands of a tyrannical, brutal husband whose cruelty had grown with the years until it became quite intolerable.

The Queen might in fact have continued to endure her unhappiness if it had not been for Ilona.

The King in his fanatical rages knocked his wife about and often to relieve his feelings had beaten her almost insensible. But when he attacked his daughter, the Queen, quiet, gentle, and, as he imagined, utterly subservient to his will, rebelled.

She had said nothing. She had merely asked permission to visit her parents in Budapest.

As her father was growing old and was reported to be ill, it was impossible for the King to refuse such a request.

Once in Hungary, the Queen had written, saying that she had no intention of returning to the purgatory that her life had become.

She had been forced to leave her son behind her,

17

but that was inevitable because at seventeen Prince Julius had started his Army career and it would have been impossible for him to desert his Regiment.

But the Queen had carried Ilona to safety.

Because she feared that her husband's reaction might be to injure her parents, she left Budapest.

The Queen's father and mother were of Royal blood but they were impoverished. Their lands had been taken from them by the Austrians.

They had nothing left but their pride and their self-respect and she could not allow them to suffer on her account.

The Queen took Ilona, as far as her husband was concerned, to an unknown destination.

They had in fact moved across Europe until they reached Paris, where the Queen had a few friends. They were all older than she was, but they were quiet, intelligent people who welcomed her amongst them.

She had also thought to find in Paris the kind of education that she believed was essential for her daughter.

Ilona had attended one of the famous Convents, where she was accepted as an ordinary pupil and no-one had the slightest idea of her rank.

As Madame Radák, the Queen, with the little money she owned herself and which had been settled on her by her parents, rented a small house in a quiet street off the Champs Élysées and settled down to lead a normal life.

It had been a relief to know that she was free of the mental and physical torture that had been an inescapable terror during the years of her marriage.

She taught Ilona that self-control was a sign of good breeding and character.

The manner in which the King had treated his wife left an indelible mark on her.

But the Queen was determined that Ilona should be made to forget all she had seen and heard in the Palace at Dabrozka.

She wanted her to acquire a serenity that came from a life where she met decent, civilised people who behaved as might be expected of their noble blood.

The ancient Comtes and Comtesses and the Marquises and Abbes who made up the small number of acquaintances that the Queen had in Paris were all aristocrats of the old school.

Their manners were impeccable. If they were unhappy they hid it behind a smiling mask; if they suffered either physically or mentally, it was buried beneath their pride.

Because she had suffered so greatly from her husband's outbursts of temper, and because she had found it impossible to assuage his violence, the Queen had instilled into Ilona her own creed.

It was that never under any circumstances must one's emotions, whatever they might be, show themselves in front of others.

It hurt her occasionally when she would see beneath the veneer she was trying to impart to her daughter the passionate emotions of a Dabrozkan bursting through.

When the Dabrozkans loved they loved, when they hated they hated. There were no half measures, no "grey" in-between state of indifference when they did not care!

A Dabrozkan was positive, a Dabrozkan was ardent, jealous, vengeful, and wildly ecstatic in love.

It was this part of her daughter's blood that the Queen was determined to eradicate or at least hold completely under control.

Ilona was therefore taught not to express herself too enthusiastically, not to kiss too effusively, nor to show too much affection for her toys or her playmates.

"Remember you are Royal! Remember how the French aristocrats went to the guillotine with a smile on their lips, joking with each other even as they laid their heads under the sharp knife."

"But I am not likely to be guillotined, Mama!" Ilona had remonstrated.

"There are other things in life that are worse," the Queen had said enigmatically, "and whatever they may be, Ilona, you will face them with courage, without complaining, and without letting anyone know what you may be suffering inside you."

19

That was the way her mother had died, Ilona thought.

At times the Queen must have been in an agony of pain, and yet while she looked paler every day she had never revealed her suffering, not even to the Doctor!

When Ilona had found her dead she was lying on her back with her hands clasped over her breast, a faint smile on her lips, as if by her very attitude she defied death itself.

On her mother's death, it had seemed to Ilona that the bottom had fallen out of her world, and she faced a desolation and loneliness so frightening that she wanted to scream at the horror of it.

But because she knew what her mother expected of her, she told all the old friends who called to offer their condolences that she was "all right."

'Somehow,' she thought, 'I will make arrangements for the future, and there is no reason to burden others with my troubles.'

Only to old Magda, her mother's maid, who had been with them ever since they had left Dabrozka, did she ask despairingly:

"What shall we do, Magda? Where shall we go? We cannot stay here forever."

She almost felt as if the little house in Paris had become a tomb from which her mother had escaped, leaving her inside.

Her only contact with the world was with the old aristocrats whom her mother had loved but who in fact were a generation older.

Two of them had died already in the Siege of Paris, which had been responsible for her mother's death also, and those who were left were old and very frail, and not likely to live long.

"What shall I do? Where shall I go?" Ilona had asked herself frequently night after night.

Then fate had answered the question for her.

She was alone in the house, because Magda had gone out shopping, when a knock had come at the front door.

She wondered who it could be at such an early

hour of the morning, then told herself it could be none of their friends and must therefore be a trades-man.

But it was unlike Magda to have anything sent to the house.

She always insisted on going herself to market, to choose the best food they could afford and to bargain fiercely over every centime.

Ilona had gone to the door to find outside two elder-ly gentlemen, one of whom said:

"We wish to speak with Her Royal Highness, the Princess Ilona of Dabrozka!"

For a moment it was difficult for Ilona to realise that they spoke of herself.

She had not been a Royal Princess for the eight years that she had been abroad with her mother.

Mademoiselle Ilona Radák was of no importance in Paris, and the high-sounding title not only surprised her but made her feel a little quiver of apprehension.

"Why do you wish to see the Princess?" she asked evasively.

"She is at home?" one of the gentleman asked.

She knew by the expression on his face and the note in his voice that he had been worried in case they had come to the wrong address.

With difficulty Ilona remembered her manners.

"Will you please come in, *Messieurs?*"

She led them into the small Salon where her moth-er's few treasures, which she had inherited from her parents, were arranged against the grey-panelled walls and the Louis XIV furniture was covered in a faded blue brocade.

Despite the fact that she herself had opened the door, there was something in her bearing that told the gentlemen who she was.

"You are Her Royal Highness?" one of them asked.

"I am!" Ilona had replied, and knew as she spoke that a new chapter in her life was beginning.

* * *

Now as she rode up the last incline towards the front door of the Palace she remembered clearly the look of satisfaction in the gentlemen's eyes.

They both were, she learnt, Ministers of State in her father's Government in Dabrozka.

They had been sent to find her, having had no idea that her mother was not still alive.

"Your brother, His Royal Highness Prince Julius, is dead!" said the one who she later learnt was the Foreign Secretary.

"I am . . . sorry," she said automatically. "How did he . . . die?"

She thought the Foreign Secretary hesitated before he replied:

"It was—an accident. The Prince was involved in a fight that took place at an Inn."

He paused before he went on:

"No-one quite knows how it started, but it was late at night and some of the gentlemen had dined rather well."

It seemed to Ilona a useless way for Julius, who was so gay and dashing, to die.

She remembered him as always laughing, always riding more dangerously and more wildly than any other young men of his age.

It was impossible to think of him as still and lifeless.

But there was nothing she could say.

She merely waited to hear why two Statesmen from Dabrozka should call on her.

"We have come," the Foreign Secretary continued, "because there is now no male Heir to the Throne. His Majesty wishes you to take your brother's place."

Ilona had stared incredulously.

"My . . . brother's . . . place?"

"On your father's death you will become the Ruler of Dabrozka."

"N-no . . . no, I could not . . . do that!" she cried.

Even as Ilona spoke she thought her protestations showed a lack of self-control and knew how much her mother would have disapproved.

With an effort she said quietly:

"Perhaps you will explain it to me a little more fully."

It was just a question of words, she thought later. She really had no choice in the matter, and she was quite certain that had she refused to accompany the

Statesmen they would have found other means of persuading her to do as her father wished.

Underlying the courteous request that she should accompany them back to Dabrozka was a Royal Command, which had to be obeyed.

She had the feeling that they had expected her mother to refuse to return.

But even so, she herself would have been obliged to do what they asked of her, for the simple reason that her father was her natural guardian by the laws of Dabrozka, as indeed by the laws of any country.

He could therefore insist, should he wish to do so, on having his daughter with him.

Moreover, Ilona was not certain that she wished to refuse.

There was something fascinating in the thought of returning home after all these years.

She was well aware how much her mother had feared her father. She could remember being terrified of him as a child and hiding from him in terror after he had beaten her.

But now, she told herself, she was grown up.

'I will return to Dabrozka,' she thought, 'and if I cannot bear it, then I will run away, just as Mama did.'

She had the idea, however, that escape might not be so easy a second time.

Her grandparents had been dead for some years, so she would not be able to use them as an excuse to go to Budapest.

But, with the optimism of youth, she was certain that if she made up her mind to do so she would find a way to return to Paris.

The question was, would she want to leave?

After the recent months of misery and loneliness since her mother's death, she was glad to have a chance to forget the horror and privations of the Siege.

'Papa did not worry about us then,' she thought.

But because she wished to be fair, she told herself it had not been his fault that they had left the peace and plenty of Dabrozka for France, which after the disastrous defeat at Sedan had been invaded by the Prussians.

Even to think of those terrifying months when food became shorter and shorter, fuel was almost unobtainable, and Paris was bombarded was to make Ilona shiver.

Then she told herself that her mother had not complained, and she would be very cowardly if she trembled now over what was past history.

Could anything, she had asked herself, be worse than the Siege?

Dabrozka seemed in retrospect a land of light and loveliness, and she had known as she journeyed towards it with the two Statesmen that she was not apprehensive of the future, but merely excited at what it might bring her.

Now Ilona could see the servants waiting for her at the door of the Palace.

She turned to the Colonel and said quietly:

"Thank you for taking me on a most interesting and enjoyable ride. I think it would be a mistake to mention that my horse bolted with me. If my father is apprehensive about my safety, he might curtail my riding."

"It will not be mentioned, Your Royal Highness," the Colonel replied.

His eyes met hers and she gave a little smile, knowing that they understood each other perfectly.

At the same time, as the footmen helped her down she wondered what the Colonel or anyone else would say if they knew what had really happened during what should have been a sedate morning's ride.

She had been kissed!

Kissed by a strange man who was obviously part of a band of discontented and dissident peasants, a man who had treated her both insolently and familiarly.

A man whose lips, hard and possessive, she could still feel on hers!

Chapter Two

Once in the Palace, Ilona went up to her bed-room, where she found Magda waiting for her.

She had already been told by the servants that her father required her presence, but she wished first to bathe and change after riding, and Magda had everything ready for her.

When they were alone in the huge bed-room that had been used by her mother when she was Queen, Ilona said:

"Did you know, Magda, that the gypsies have been told to leave Dabrozka?"

"I learnt of it as soon as I arrived, *M'mselle*," Magda answered.

She was an elderly woman with grey hair and a kind, understanding face.

It was to Magda that the Queen had entrusted her daughter when she fled from Dabrozka, and Magda had been their mainstay, their confidant, and their friend all the years they had been in exile.

Ilona often thought that if it had not been for Magda they would have starved to death in the Siege of Paris.

But somehow, by some magic means of her own, Magda had managed to produce food of some sort, even though it was often nothing more than a loaf of bread.

Now, as Magda helped Ilona out of her riding-habit, the old maid went on:

"There's hard feelings in the Palace and I'm told over the whole of the land about His Majesty's decree."

"How can Papa do anything so cruel and unreasonable?" Ilona cried.

Even as she asked the question she knew the answer: her father was never anything else!

They had talked so often of the miseries the gypsies had suffered in Romania and how a great number of them had escaped from the bondage in which they had belonged body and soul to the great Hospodars or war-chiefs.

Braving the snows, they had somehow managed to climb the mountains into Dabrozka. Many had died on the way, but those who had survived had terrible tales to tell of their servitude.

They had received no wage and the only food they were allowed was small portions of mamaliga or Indian corn, helped out with some sunflower-seeds.

When punished they were flogged naked and iron bars were fixed round their necks to prevent them from sleeping.

The King of Dabrozka at that time had welcomed them as he had welcomed those from Hungary who were almost as cruelly treated by Queen Maria Thérèsa.

She had prohibited them from sleeping in tents, electing their own Chiefs, using their own language, and being married if they had not the means to support a family.

The gypsy men were pressed into Military service, the children often taken away by soldiers to places where their parents never saw them again.

Ilona's mother had read her a horrifying report written by a woman who had travelled through Central Europe at the time:

Pickets of soldiers appeared in all parts of Hungary where there were gypsies and took away their children, including those who were just weaned, and young married couples still wearing their wedding finery.

The despair of these unfortunate people cannot be described. The parents clung to the vehicles that were carrying off their children, only to be beaten off with blows from batons and rifle-butts. Some immediately committed suicide.

But in Dabrozka the gypsies had settled down and become a part of the community. Their music, their dancing, and their singing were all interwoven with the ordinary life of the Dabrozkans.

"Why," Ilona asked now, "has Papa turned against the gypsies? Where will they go if they have to leave here?"

"From all I have heard," Magda answered, lowering her voice, "they have merely moved into Sáros land, where the Prince has offered them his protection."

"No wonder Papa is incensed with him!" Ilona remarked.

She could imagine nothing that would infuriate her father more than that the gypsies should defy him by remaining in Dabrozka under the protection of the man he considered his enemy.

"The people are not happy, *M'mselle*," Magda said. "We have returned to a sad place, a land of weeping."

Ilona did not reply. It was what she herself had thought.

When she dried herself after her bath and started to dress, she wondered if it would be possible for her to talk to her father of such matters.

Surely he could not wish to rule over land from which the laughter had gone?

She had the feeling, however, that she would not be brave enough to say anything that would anger him.

He had been unusually pleasant in the short time since she had returned to the Palace, even though he had grumbled at the Statesmen who had escorted her from Paris, saying that they had taken too long on the journey.

The delay was due to the fact that Ilona could not leave Paris until she had bought herself some new clothes.

When she had realised that she had no alternative but to return to her own country, she had said to the Foreign Secretary:

"When would you wish us to leave, *Monsieur?*"

She found it difficult to address him in any other way. She had grown so used in the last eight years to saying *Madame* or *Monsieur* to everyone to whom she spoke that it came automatically to her lips.

It was just the same with Magda, who she was certain would never remember to call her anything but "*M'mselle* Ilona."

"We wish to leave immediately, Your Royal Highness," the Foreign Secretary had replied, "but there is one thing I must mention."

"What is that?" Ilona asked.

"His Majesty would not expect you to be wearing black!"

"But that is because His Majesty did not know that my mother is dead, and I am in mourning," Ilona replied.

"You have my deepest condolences," the Foreign Secretary replied, "but nevertheless I would not be doing my duty if I did not impress upon you that it would be impossible for you to arrive in Dabrozka wearing the gown you have on."

"But why, *Monsieur?* Will you not explain your reason for making such a statement?" Ilona enquired curiously.

"His Majesty has decided that too much time is wasted on funerals and the tending of graves," the Foreign Secretary replied.

"Too much time?" Ilona exclaimed.

"Yes, Your Royal Highness. He has therefore closed the Church-yards, and once people have been buried they may no longer be visited by their relatives."

"I have never heard anything so absurd!" Ilona declared.

"It is His Majesty's decree: no Dabrozkan is allowed to show any sign of mourning by wearing black, and the Prayers for the Dead have been deleted from the Church Services."

Ilona sat very still.

She was horrified at what she had heard. At the same time, to express her feelings too forcibly would, she knew, be considered by her mother to be over-emotional.

After all, she reasoned with herself, although she

missed her mother unbearably, she was certain that she was not dead.

More than once when she had been alone she had felt that her mother was near her and knew that her love still encompassed her.

"I have few clothes," she said aloud, "and the only new ones I possess are black. What little money my mother and I had during the Siege of Paris was required to buy food."

"I was empowered by His Majesty before we left to purchase anything you require," the Foreign Secretary replied. "I therefore suggest that Your Royal Highness furnish yourself with everything you need."

Ilona thanked him politely but there was an irrepressible little gleam of excitement in her eyes.

What woman could resist, after years of pinching and saving, being able to buy without any restrictions the delectable, smart, elaborate gowns for which Paris was famous?

She started out early the next morning with Magda and they visited all the great Couturiers who until now had only been names to her.

During the years she had been in Paris it would have been impossible for Ilona not to know of the extravagance, the luxury, and the exotic splendour that had flourished during the reign of Louis Napoleon.

The Empress Eugénie had set the fashion in a dozen different ways—by wearing the first crinoline, which had astounded and beguiled the male population, and by ordering velvet from Lyons and lace from Normandy.

She created employment for thousands of workers in the silk, cotton, and feather trades, besides encouraging Jewellers, Hatters, Silversmiths, and tradesmen of every sort.

Even at the Convent the girls had talked of the huge parties given at the Tuileries Palace and in every great Mansion in Paris.

What is more, Ilona would have been blind when she rode in the Bois if she had not noticed Ladies who were certainly not aristocrats but who drove behind the finest and most expensive horses, and whose costumes and jewellery made them look like glittering birds of Paradise!

"Such women are a disgrace!" Magda had declared.

But Ilona had thought them very pretty and colourful.

Because she felt that her father owed her something for all the years of obscurity, for the privation and suffering she and her mother had endured during the siege, Ilona bought herself an entire trousseau.

There were gowns for evening, gowns for afternoon, for morning, and for every other possible occasion.

There were wraps edged with swan's-down or fur, embroidered with sequins and gold thread.

There were hats trimmed with feathers, flowers, and ribbons to perch on top of her head, and small sunshades decorated to match, edged with real lace.

She bought shoes, gloves, and reticules, and silk stockings and underclothes that were of such fine silk that they would have easily passed through a ring.

It was all a delight and an excitement she had never expected and when finally she looked in the mirror she found it hard to recognise herself.

Never before had she recognised the beauty of her dark red-gold hair, which she had inherited from her mother.

Never before had she been aware that her skin was so white and that her eyes in certain lights were a definite shade of green.

Her small waist and her curved breasts had never been seen to advantage in the gowns of cheap materials that were all her mother could afford.

She had seen the admiration in the Foreign Secretary's eyes and those of the gentleman with him when they had called, as arranged, to escort her to the Railway Station.

There were huge trunks of clothes filling up the hall of the tiny house, but Ilona told them that they contained only a part of her purchases, and the rest when they were ready would be sent on to her.

She knew that the Foreign Secretary had looked

slightly shocked when he glanced at the great sheaf of bills that she presented to him.

But she told herself that if she was to revert to her Royal rank, at least she must be dressed as befitted a Princess.

What she would hardly dare admit to herself was that her new clothes gave her confidence.

She had a feeling that to return to her father's protection looking shabby and poverty-stricken would be almost an invitation for him to crush her, to make her feel subservient and even more afraid of him than she was already.

"I will not let him know that I am frightened," Ilona told herself a hundred times as the train carried her away from Paris towards a new life.

She was old enough now to realise what her mother had suffered before she had, with almost incredible daring, left her husband and refused to return.

The Queen had been certain that had the King been able to find her he would have dragged her back to Dabrozka by force.

But they had covered their tracks well and the Queen's close friends would never have betrayed her.

Dabrozka was such a small country that it was not of much interest to those who lived in Western Europe. Yet in its own way it was of great political importance because of its independence.

It had been left alone by the Turks when they had extended their Empire from Greece to the boundaries of Romania; when the Austrians had subdued Hungary, they had ignored Dabrozka.

Perhaps its almost impregnable barrier of high mountains had something to do with it, besides the fact that the Dabrozkans were known to be fearless and ferocious fighters.

Whatever the reason, Dabrozka, with its precipitous mountain passes, deep gorges, and smiling valleys, was still an independent State with its own Monarchy and its own age-old customs.

As Magda finished fastening the exquisite gown of pale green silk, which reminded Ilona of the grass on the steppe, she walked to the window to look out at the incredible view.

From the heights of the Palace she could see for many miles over the surrounding country.

Yet through some freak of fate the Sáros land, which her father so detested, was nearer than most other parts of his Kingdom.

The river that lay below passed through the centre of the Capital of the country, Vitózi.

On this side of it, Ilona could see the Cathedral, the Houses of Parliament, and a large number of impressive Municipal Buildings.

On the other side lay both the rich and the poorer residential part of the city.

There were white Villas surrounded by colourful gardens and narrow streets flanked with high wooden houses.

Beyond them, half hidden amongst the trees, were the peasants' huts, built of straw but nevertheless picturesque with their small-holdings in which they kept their sheep, pigs, and goats.

And beyond the city, high on a hill, and yet by no means as high as the Palace, was Sáros Castle, the home of the Princes of Sáros for centuries of time.

She could just see its towers and turrets above the trees and the flag of its owner fluttering in the breeze.

It looked very picturesque, for behind it rose one of the highest mountains of the Kingdom and down one side there ran a huge waterfall that after a torrent of rain would be haloed by a rainbow.

The rich, undulating valley and the wooded slopes all lay below Ilona in the brilliant sunshine.

Nothing, she knew, could be more fertile than the valleys, which, protected by the mountains from the cold winds of Russia, could grow amazing crops that would make any country prosperous.

And yet, unfairly and without a thought for justice, her father had imposed the penal taxes of which the Colonel had spoken.

Ilona was certain that it would be impossible for the peasants to give away half their harvest and yet have enough left for themselves.

"I shall have to speak about it to Papa," she told herself.

But although the words were brave she knew the mere thought of encountering his anger was enough to make her shiver with fear.

"You are ready, *M'mselle?*" Magda asked. "It would be best not to keep His Majesty waiting too long."

"You are right, Magda, as usual," Ilona said with a smile.

She bent to kiss the old maid, adding:

"Do not look so worried. Even if I am five minutes late he cannot eat me!"

Yet when she walked down the Great Staircase with her hand on the gold bannister she felt apprehensive.

But she showed no sign of her fears when a footman in the Royal Livery opened the door of the Salon where she knew her father would be waiting for her.

He was standing at the far end of the room in front of a large stone fireplace that in the winter burnt logs as thick as beer-barrels.

As she walked slowly towards him with the frills of her bustle rustling behind her over the carpet, she had to admit that he was both very impressive and still an extremely handsome man.

He had the square forehead and clear-cut features that were characteristic of the Dabrozkans, and while his hair was grey his thick eye-brows were still dark over his deep-set eyes, and his chin was square beneath his long moustache.

He did not speak until Ilona was nearly at his side. Then he asked harshly:

"Where the devil have you been? I sent for you an hour ago!"

"I am sorry, Papa, to have kept you waiting," Ilona replied, "but I told you that I was going riding and I did not learn that you desired to see me until my return."

"You should have come to me as soon as you arrived back at the Palace," the King said.

"I wished to change," Ilona replied, "and I wished also, Papa, to show you one of my new gowns from Paris. I hope you admire it."

She turned round as if to let him see the full beauty

of the gown with its bustle of cunningly contrived frills, and the tightness of the bodice, which gave her such an exquisite figure.

"I have no time for such frivolities," the King said impatiently. "There is a Deputation here to see me and I have kept them cooling their heels until you condescended to appear."

Ilona raised her eye-brows.

"A Deputation, Papa? What do they want?"

"God knows! I expect they wish to complain. I seldom hear anything else! But if you are to take Julius's place, then you had better be present when I grant them an audience."

Ilona was silent for a moment.

She had found it difficult to believe what her father had meant when he told her on her arrival in Dabrozka what her position was to be.

"Your brother is dead," he had said abruptly. "Killed by those Sáros devils on whom one day I shall wreak revenge for their crime."

He spoke with such violence that Ilona replied:

"I understood that Julius died by accident, Papa."

"Accident? When was the death of the Heir to a Throne ever an accident?" the King roared. "It was premeditated murder, and one day I will kill Aladár Sáros as he killed my son!"

"Is it to tell me this that you brought me back from Paris?" Ilona asked.

"No, of course not!" the King had answered. "I brought you back to take your brother's place!"

He had seen the worried expression in Ilona's eyes and continued:

"I have to have an heir and he must be a Radák. Because your mother was such a weakling and no fit wife for a robust man, she gave me only two children."

Ilona had clenched her fingers together at the insult to her mother, but because she knew she must control her feelings she had managed to say in an expressionless tone:

"Will you explain, Papa, exactly what you expect of me?"

"You will prepare yourself to reign over this country on my death," the King answered. "Not that I am thinking of dying as yet, but I was training Julius and now that he has gone I must train you!"

As if the idea upset him, the King kicked over a stool and as it crashed to the floor he said harshly:

"God knows what a woman will do on the Throne, but at least you are my own flesh and blood, and there is no-one else I can trust."

He had gone on to abuse violently Prince Aladár and all those who supported him.

He was working himself up into one of his rages, which, Ilona remembered only too well, were usually a prelude to violent action of some sort.

Somehow she managed to mollify him and make him talk more sensibly about the country and the manner in which he wished it governed.

She wished now that she knew more about what he had done and why he had suddenly passed new laws.

'Surely,' she thought to herself, 'someone could have convinced him that they would cause so much suffering and resentment?'

Aloud, however, she said demurely:

"I shall be very honoured, Papa, to accompany you to receive the Deputation. Have you informed them of my arrival?"

"Informed them? Why should I?" the King asked in a loud voice. "They will find out soon enough. Everything that happens in this damned valley is talked about as if it was shouted from the tops of the mountains!"

That was true, Ilona thought, and she was quite certain that soon everyone in Dabrozka would be aware that she had returned home.

What she had meant was: Had the Prime Minister and his Government been told of her new position?

At the same time, she was well aware that, having told her she was to be his heir, her father was quite capable of changing his mind.

Her mother had told her often enough how unpredictable he could be in every way.

His friend today was his enemy tomorrow; a public

appearance arranged months ahead would be cancelled at the last minute.

"It all caused so much unnecessary trouble and distress," the Queen had said almost pathetically. "That is why, Ilona, you must always keep your word. You must never go back on a promise. Your integrity must never be in question."

"Come along! Come along!" the King was saying sharply. "If we have to see these blasted people let us get it over. I have something better to do than listen to their whining and their ever-lasting petitions!"

Ilona followed him across the Salon.

When they entered the Great Hall with its ancient weapons decorating the walls and its flags hanging from the bannisters, they turned down a wide corridor that led to the Throne-Room.

It was a very impressive room, rebuilt by her grandfather, who had taken as a model the Hall of Mirrors at Versailles.

The long windows that looked out over the formal gardens were reflected and rereflected in the mirrors on either side of the room, and the crystal glass candelabra and the gold embroidered curtains were exquisite.

Not far from the door through which they had entered stood a dais on which there were two extremely impressive Thrones.

They were of gold set with amethysts and carnelians, all mined in the Dabrozkan mountains, and mounted by a canopy emblazoned with the same precious stones.

The Queen's Throne was a smaller replica of the King's, and Ilona, following her father onto the dais, knew without asking that that was where he wished her to sit.

As soon as he had seated himself she sat down, holding her back very straight, aware that the frilled train of her gown curved elegantly beside her.

She looked with interest at the men standing in front of them.

The spokesman who stood a little in front of the

others was, she was certain, the Prime Minister, and she knew his name was Andreas Fülek.

All the Statesmen, and there were a dozen of them, bowed low to the King before Andreas Fülek said:

"We have asked to see Your Majesty on a matter of great importance."

"You always say that," the King growled.

The Prime Minister was not much older than forty, Ilona decided. He was not a tall man but he bore himself proudly.

She had the feeling, even before she heard his quiet voice, that he was not afraid of her father as most people were.

She could see the other Statesmen eyeing the King nervously and she was quite sure they were speculating as to what mood he was likely to be in and if their petition had any chance of being successful.

"We have come into possession, Sire," the Prime Minister went on, "of some extremely alarming information with regard to the intentions of the Russians towards our country."

"What do you mean—you have come into possession of information?" the King asked contemptuously. "Tell the truth, man, and say that what you have heard came from your gypsy spies, that scum you employ to tell you tales that have no substance in fact."

"What we have learnt, Sire, does not come on this occasion from the gypsies, although they have warned us in the past of what was being said across the border."

"And what is being said?" the King enquired.

"The Russians intend to exploit to their own advantage the difficulties that exist in our country."

"What difficulties? What are you talking about?" the King demanded.

"I am referring to the enmity that is almost a state of war, Sire, existing between the Radáks and the Sáros."

"Good God! Did you imagine I was not aware of it?" the king ejaculated. "If you want the truth, Prime Minister, it *is* a state of war! I intend to destroy those who do not obey my laws and who flaunt my authority to the point of letting loose my prisoners!"

"That policy is exactly what the Russians are hoping for," the Prime Minister said quietly.

The King glared at him but did not speak, and the Prime Minister went on:

"I have unmistakable evidence, Sire, that they have infiltrated our people and are stirring up the trouble-makers with gifts of money and the promise of many benefits if the Monarchy be overthrown."

"You are crazy!" the King said. "Who is likely to overthrow me?"

"A civil war is what the Russians are encouraging, Sire," the Prime Minister explained. "That would furnish a sufficient excuse for the Russian Armies to march in, on the pretext of keeping order."

Ilona gave a little gasp.

"Your Majesty is aware that should they invade this country when everything is at peace," the Prime Minister continued, "both the Austro-Hungarian Empire and Romania would protest and might even actively support us."

He paused and his eyes were on the King as he said slowly:

"But if we continue to fight amongst ourselves, if the country remains divided as it is at the moment, the Russians will take control. Once they are in power, it would be extremely difficult to dislodge them."

The King leant back in his chair, his under-lip thrown forward in an ugly expression of disbelief.

But Ilona knew that he was genuinely surprised at what the Prime Minister had said.

She was quite certain that it was a reasonable and plausible forecast of what would happen.

For years she had been told that the Russians coveted Dabrozka.

Actually, the mountains on the Eastern side of the country where it bordered Russia were not very far from the Capital and were more negotiable than those on the boundaries of Hungary and Romania.

Also, Russia was very large and her Army was enormous!

If it came to war, Ilona was certain that however

brave the Dabrozkans might be they would be over-whelmed by sheer numbers.

The Prime Minister broke the silence.

"In the Council this morning, Sire, we found a solution!"

"A solution?" the King echoed. "What might that be?"

He still spoke in an aggressive manner, but although there was no outward evidence of it Ilona was certain that he was in fact seriously perturbed by what he had been told.

"We all have heard," the Prime Minister went on, "of Her Royal Highness's return."

He bowed to Ilona as he said:

"May I welcome you back, Princess? And may I say in the years that you have been away you have been greatly missed? Your beauty and your charm will, I know, open a new era in the history of our country."

Ilona smiled at him.

"Thank you, Prime Minister," she answered. "I am very grateful for your kind words and I wish I could in some way bring you peace."

To her surprise, every man in the Delegation turned his eyes towards her and there was an expression on their faces that she could not understand.

"Peace is what we have prayed you would bring us, and which is within your power to give," the Prime Minister said.

Ilona looked at him in astonishment and the King said sharply:

"What the hell are you talking about? I make neither head nor tail of it! If you have a solution, as you say, then let us hear it."

"Our solution, Sire, is very simple," the Prime Minister answered. "It is that this country, which we all love so much and which we all wish to serve, should be united and there should be no more fighting, no more dissention, between the Radáks and the Sáros."

"And how do you hope to achieve that?" the King asked, sneering.

"By the marriage of Her Royal Highness Princess Ilona to Prince Aladár Sáros!"

For a moment there was an almost deathly silence.

Then as Ilona gave a little gasp her father sat forward, hammering with a clenched fist on the golden arm of his chair.

"Do you call that a solution?" he yelled. "Can you really consider that I would give my only child, my daughter, to that devil who has defied me, murdered my son, and incited my own people against me?"

His voice seemed to echo and re-echo round the Hall of Mirrors.

The Prime Minister said quietly after a moment:

"If that is your final word, Sire, then we may as well open the passes to the Russians and welcome them as our conquerors!"

Again there was silence.

Ilona felt her heart beating violently, and although she hoped no-one noticed it she clenched her fingers together on her lap.

She tightened them as they were interlocked so that the hard pressure prevented her from crying out.

'It is impossible!' she thought.

Impossible that they should actually be asking her to marry a man she had never seen, a man of whom she knew nothing except that her father loathed him.

In Paris everyone had discussed love; the girls at the Convent had giggled about men and talked of being married as if when it happened they would move into some special Paradise.

Ilona had not listened to them very attentively.

But now she knew she had thought that someday she might fall in love, and since she was no longer a person of any particular importance she would not have to submit to an arranged marriage.

It was usual in France, she knew, but she was not French.

She had read and listened to the Hungarian legends and stories of lovers who defied the whole world and found a rapturous happiness.

Without discussing it with her mother or indeed mentioning it to anyone, Ilona had decided that she would never marry until she fell in love.

She had a child-like confidence, despite their quiet way of life, that one day a man whom she could love and who loved her would come into her life.

She had always imagined him coming to her like a crusading Knight riding a fiery half-tamed horse over the green steppes and nothing would matter but their ecstatic love for each other.

But from such romantic dreams she was suddenly awakened to harsh reality.

She understood all too well what the Prime Minister was saying.

She knew without his elaborating on the subject that it would in fact be the only way for Dabrozka to find peace.

"But why must it be me?" she asked herself despairingly.

It was a question men and women had asked since the beginning of time when they were confronted with a personal issue of the heart.

The answer was quite simple.

There was no-one else!

Her father had already chosen her as the Heir to the Throne of Dabrozka.

Prince Aladár Sáros, although he was not Royal, wielded in his own territory power and authority equal to that of the Monarchy.

There was no other way by which the feuds, the enmity, and the hatreds of the divided country could be dissolved.

"I will not agree!" the King said stubbornly.

"Well well, Your Majesty," the Prime Minister said briskly. "In that case, we can only withdraw to await the arrival of our enemies."

"How can you be so sure that this is what the Russians are planning?" the King enquired.

"We have, as Your Majesty knows, our agents in Russia, besides the gypsies, whom you despise," the Prime Minister replied.

"You can rely upon their information?"

"What they have told us has been confirmed in a dozen different ways," the Prime Minister replied.

"The trouble-makers we have arrested in the city have, when they were questioned, confirmed our suspicions one hundred percent!"

The King was silent. Then one of the Delegation said tentatively:

"Would it not be in order, Sire, to ask the Princess if she would be prepared to save her country?"

Again everybody's eyes turned towards Ilona, and she had the feeling that her father too was waiting for her answer.

For a moment she felt she must cry out her repudiation of such an idea and the horror that it gave her.

Then she remembered her mother and the teaching that had been instilled in her from childhood.

"We must always trust God to guide us to do what is right," the Queen had said. "We are not wise or clever enough to decide great problems for ourselves. God always knows best."

"Did God think it right that you should leave Papa?" Ilona had asked.

"I prayed about it for many years," her mother answered. "Not a day passed when I did not go down on my knees and ask for God's guidance."

She gave a sigh that seemed to come from the very depths of her being.

"I thought, in fact I was sure, that God wanted me to do my duty. I was married to your father. I had taken the vows of obedience and I intended to fulfill them."

"What happened, Mama?" Ilona asked.

"When your father beat you for some quite minor offence until you became unconscious, I knew as if I heard a voice speak from Heaven that I must take you away to safety."

She made a little gesture as she said simply:

"It was no longer a question of my duty only to my husband, but my duty towards my own child, who could not protect herself."

The Delegation was waiting, and almost as if her mother spoke for her Ilona heard her voice say quietly:

"I will do what you . . . require of me . . . if it will save . . . our country!"

There was a sound of relief that seemed to come from all twelve men standing in front of her.

"We can only thank Your Royal Highness from the very depths of our hearts," the Prime Minister said.

"And what about Aladár Sáros?" the King enquired. "Have you obtained his consent to this crazy idea? Or are you so sure he will come crawling up the hill to the Palace on all fours to get himself accepted as my son-in-law?"

There was such an unpleasant tone in her father's voice that Ilona felt ashamed.

How right her mother had been, she thought, that one should never parade one's innermost feelings and that one should keep control of one's emotions.

"It was our first duty, Sire, to put the proposition before our King before we discussed it with anyone else," the Prime Minister answered.

"Most obliging of you!" the King remarked sarcastically.

"But now, when we leave here, we will go at once to Sáros Castle. Since the Prince is deeply concerned about the position in which this country finds itself, and since he is as aware as we are of the dangers confronting us, I am certain he will agree."

"He would be a fool if he did not!" The King sneered.

The Prime Minister ignored the remark.

"There is one further point I must put before Your Majesty, and that is the importance of speed. The reports I have before me are that the Russians have already drawn up plans to enter this country within the next few days."

"How can you be sure of that?"

"We have already apprehended two men in the city carrying dynamite with which they intended to blow up Parliament, and also the bridge over the river!"

"God Almighty! What the hell are the police doing? And we have an Army!"

"It is impossible for either of the forces you mention,

43

Sire, to keep control of undesirable aliens, when they are already fully occupied in keeping our own people from each other's throats!"

There was a truth in this that the King could not gainsay and the Prime Minister went on:

"I therefore suggest, with your agreement, Sire, and Her Royal Highness's, that we arrange for the marriage to take place the day after tomorrow in order to resolve the situation as quickly as possible!"

It was with difficulty that Ilona prevented herself from crying out in denial.

It was one thing to discuss marriage with a stranger —a man she had never seen. But to be pitch-forked into it with hardly time to breathe was something she had not foreseen or imagined.

She did not speak and after a moment the King growled:

"If it has to happen I suppose there is no point in hanging about."

"Very well, Sire. If you will leave it with me I will make all the arrangements, and with the Princess's agreement the announcement will be made tonight by Criers in the Market-Place."

He glanced at Ilona as he added:

"The decorations will go up tomorrow. The Archbishop will be invited to conduct the ceremony, and the details of the celebration can be discussed later."

"God knows what we have to celebrate!" the King ejaculated.

"It is the only possible way to save Dabrozka," the Prime Minister insisted.

"Then get on with it, damn you!" the King said with a sudden burst of anger. "And get out—all of you! I do not want to see your ugly faces, knowing you are crowing over me because you think you have brought off a coup!"

He rose to his feet as he shouted:

"I warn you—no good will come of this marriage, and as far as I am concerned a million Russians would be preferable to one Sáros!"

He left the dais and stamped out of the Throne-Room.

Ilona looked at the Prime Minister. Then, feeling embarrassed and unsure of herself, she rose.

He crossed to her side and taking her hand in his raised it to his lips.

"May I thank you, Princess," he asked, "for your courage, and for showing that while you have been away from us for so long you still have your country's well-being at heart?"

"I . . . thought . . . today," Ilona said hesitatingly, "that some of the . . . happiness I remembered had . . . left our people."

"You will bring it back," the Prime Minister said reassuringly. "I am as certain of that as I am certain that you and you alone can save us."

"Is the situation really as bad as you described to the King?"

"If anything, it is worse!" the Prime Minister admitted. "His Majesty hates the gypsies, but because they pass through one country to another and because they have a kinship with other gypsies of all nationalities, we have known for the last two years what the Russians are planning."

"Russia is . . . so large and we are so . . . small," Ilona said. "Why should they want us?"

"Perhaps we are Naboth's vineyard," the Prime Minister said with a faint smile. "Anyway, we know they have been working feverishly while waiting for an opportunity to strike, and Prince Julius's death made them think that their hour had come!"

"They did not expect my father to send for me?" Ilona asked.

"I think if they ever knew of your existence, they had forgotten about it," the Prime Minister replied.

"Then my . . . my marriage will come as a surprise."

It was difficult to say the word "marriage" and it seemed to stick in her throat.

"A great surprise! And a very unwelcome one for the Russian Generals."

Then in another tone of voice the Prime Minister added:

"And now may I present to Your Royal Highness my

45

colleagues, all of whom, I know, are as grateful to you as I am for your understanding."

As they were introduced by the Prime Minister, each man in turn kissed Ilona's hand.

When she looked at them she realised they all were responsible, serious-minded men who would not have been deceived by some spurious tale of invasion unless it was true.

Then, because they had a lot to do, the Prime Minister took his Delegation away and Ilona, avoiding the rooms where she might find her father, ran up the stairs to her bed-room.

As she expected, Magda was there and she ran across the room to throw her arms round the old maid.

"Magda! Magda!" she cried. "I am to be married to a . . . man I have never . . . seen . . . whom Papa hates and who he swears killed Julius! Oh, Magda, I am afraid . . . terribly, terribly afraid!"

Chapter Three

"Will Papa see me, Magda?" Ilona asked.

"The Aide-de-Camp said the King will see no-one, *M'mselle*."

Ilona walked across the *Boudoir* that adjoined the Queen's bed-room and stood looking out the window.

Down in the valley she could see flags being hoisted in the city. They were blowing in the warm wind and silhouetted against the white buildings in brilliant patches of colour.

"It is absurd!" she said. "I must find out what is happening and what arrangements have been made for tomorrow."

Magda did not reply and Ilona knew from the expression on the old woman's face that she was worried.

"It will be all right, Magda," she said reassuringly. "I am sure it will be all right."

She was speaking as much to encourage herself as her maid, and as she spoke the fear and apprehension of what lay ahead of her mingled with the shock that she had received the night before.

After the Deputation had gone she had expected that her father would avoid her for some hours until he had recovered from his anger.

In a way, she could understand what he was feeling and how it was a humiliation, after all he had said about Prince Aladár, to be forced to accept him as a member of his family.

At the same time, Ilona felt that her father must realise that the country came first and that she herself was the person who was really making a sacrifice.

47

She tried to feel, without any conviction, that what was happening was natural and was only to be expected by one of Royal blood.

What was the difference between marrying Prince Aladár of Dabrozka or a Prince from another part of Europe?

At least he was not a foreigner and they were of the same nationality.

'I suppose it is because I have lived like a commoner for so long,' Ilona thought, 'that the idea of an arranged marriage is so terrifying.'

She admitted frankly to herself that that was how she felt, but she knew her mother would be ashamed of her if she showed any apprehension or distress to the outside world.

Perhaps in their desire to save Dabrozka she and Prince Aladár would together find a secure foundation on which to build their married life.

What made everything so difficult was that she knew nothing about him and there was in fact no-one in the Palace she could question.

She felt it would be undignified to ask for information from Colonel Ceáky or any of the other Court Officials.

What was more, she was quite certain that if they were part of her father's entourage they would have the same feelings about the Sáros as he had.

"I shall just have to wait and see," Ilona told herself with a wry smile.

At the same time, she was determined to discuss not only the Prince but also the whole history of the Sáros with her father.

It might anger him; he would doubtless be abusive and denounce the Prince as violently as he had done in the Throne-Room.

But it was best to be prepared, best to know the worst of what lay ahead, rather than remain in complete ignorance.

During the afternoon she walked in the gardens of the Palace and spent the rest of the day inspecting the rooms that she had not seen since she was a child.

She had forgotten what a magnificent Library her

grandfather, who had been a very erudite man, had collected.

Or that her great-grandfather had been interested in Greek culture and had a collection of statues, urns, and vases that she was sure would have been greatly appreciated in Paris.

Her mother's old friends would have enjoyed many of the pictures by great Masters that hung on the walls of the Salons and decorated the wide corridors.

These were also embellished with suits of armour fashioned in gold and silver, which had been worn in past centuries by the Kings of Dabrozka.

That the treasures the Palace contained were well arranged was due, Ilona knew, to her mother's good taste.

Hungarian by birth, the Queen was well read and had an exceptional knowledge of antiques.

Because of her mother's love of history, which she had imparted to her daughter, Ilona found that her tour through the Palace was almost like turning the pages of a book.

She only wished she had someone with her of whom she could ask questions, especially with regard to the lovely old Ikons that had come from Russia and of which there were a great number.

There was so much to see and so much to interest her that she realised that it was growing late and she should be thinking of dressing for dinner.

There was still no sign of her father, and she had gone to her bed-room expecting that they would dine together at the same hour as they had the previous evening.

Magda was waiting for her.

"I thought, *M'mselle*, you would like to dine in your *Boudoir* tonight rather than go downstairs to the Dining-Room."

"Am I alone?" Ilona asked. "Can I not dine with my father?"

"No, *M'mselle!*"

"Why not? Is he still angry?"

Magda hesitated before she answered:

"He has made other arrangements, *M'mselle*."

"Other arrangements?" Ilona queried. "You mean that he is dining with someone else?"

"Yes, *M'mselle!*"

There was something in the way Magda spoke that told Ilona there was something mysterious about her father's dinner-party.

"You know something that you have not told me, Magda," she said. "Why should there be a mystery about the person whom Papa has invited to dinner?"

Magda avoided her eyes.

"Don't trouble your head, *M'mselle*. You should have no knowledge of such women. They're a disgrace— that's what they are!"

Ilona remembered Magda using much the same words about the brilliantly attired ladies driving in the Bois.

She was silent for a moment, then she said quietly: "You mean that . . . Papa has a . . . a . . . lady-friend?"

"If that's what you wish to call it," Magda replied sourly. "It's what your poor mother had to suffer year after year!"

Ilona had looked at the maid with wide eyes.

Now she began to understand some of the things her mother had said inadvertently about her life before she left Dabrozka.

It was not only that the Queen had been physically assaulted, it was something deeper, which had left a scar that could never be erased.

"Women of that sort!"

Like most children, Ilona had never expected her parents to be associated with immorality.

She knew of course that the French were always writing of love and lovers, and that Louis Napoleon had a succession of mistresses who were whispered about and discussed by every Parisian high or low.

But such things had never concerned her personally, and she had never imagined that her father, however unpredictable he might be, would be attracted by any woman other than her mother.

Now she saw how naïve and foolish it was of her to expect anything else.

The Dabrozkans were a red-blooded, passionate race, and their songs, their music, and their dancing were all as fiery and as temperamental as their horses.

But that her father . . . !

Sternly she told herself that no man, certainly not a Dabrozkan, could be expected to live the life of a monk.

Also, she could not imagine what sort of woman would put up with her father's rages and capricious behaviour, even though he was a King.

It was however something she could not discuss with Magda.

"You are quite right, Magda!" she said aloud. "I would much prefer to dine in my *Boudoir*. I have a book to read which I am finding extremely interesting."

She found it difficult to sleep after she went to bed.

She kept thinking of her father and the woman with whom he was dining.

She suspected, although she would rather die than ask questions, that the mistress of the King would doubtless have apartments in the Palace.

It was certainly large enough to accommodate a whole Harem, if necessary. But to Ilona it was intolerable to think that she was sleeping under the same roof as an improper woman who was taking the place of her sweet and gentle mother.

However, when daylight came she told herself sharply that it was none of her business.

Her father's private life was no concern of hers. All she must think about was the safety of Dabrozka.

Her mother would have considered it her duty to save the country to which she belonged, and, if it was humanly possible, to bring peace to its people.

"I want to hear them sing and laugh again," Ilona told herself.

She was determined before she was married that she would discuss with her father the burden of the new taxes, and also the ban on mourning and the closure of the Church-yards.

From the history-books she had read with her mother she had learnt that in many countries it was often some quite small grievance that inflamed the populace and brought them to a state of revolt.

'The people must hate Papa!' she thought. 'For they cannot tend the graves or hear the Priests praying that their loved ones when they die may find eternal rest.'

She felt as if she was being given strength to fight against such injustices, and that when the time came to approach her father she would not be afraid to do so.

The difficulty was to see him at all.

She had sent a message early in the morning by Magda, asking when they could meet.

This was the third time Magda had gone to the King's apartments only to be told that His Majesty had no desire to see his daughter.

'I wish now I had gone riding,' Ilona thought.

Then irresistibly the memory came back to her of what had occurred yesterday.

It had been impossible, even with so many other problems on her mind, not to remember the feeling when she had been kissed and the hard possessiveness of the stranger's lips.

"I must forget it," Ilona had told herself in the darkness. "It was an outrage! An impertinence that only happened because I was foolish enough to run away from those who were protecting me."

She would never have contemplated riding in Paris without being accompanied by a groom; but she had imagined that in the wild Dabrozkan countryside she would be quite safe, only to find that she had been mistaken.

"Why do you not go for a walk in the garden, *M'mselle?*" Magda asked.

"I wish to see my father," Ilona replied, "and I intend to make him talk to me."

She walked determinedly towards the door.

"Put out all the white gowns we have brought from Paris, Magda," she ordered. "We have to decide which one I will wear tomorrow."

"I have already done so, *M'mselle*. There is one that I'm sure you'll think is the most beautiful."

"I will see it when I return," Ilona replied.

She walked down the Grand Staircase and along the corridors that led to the King's Reception-Room.

In the Ante-Room, Colonel Ceáky was on duty and Ilona was glad to see him.

"Good-morning, Colonel!" she said.

"Good-morning, Your Royal Highness."

"I have asked three times to see my father. I consider it important that we should discuss the arrangements for tomorrow."

"I can tell Your Royal Highness what they are," Colonel Ceáky replied.

He walked to a desk in the room as he spoke and picked up a piece of paper.

"Is there any reason why I should not discuss them with the King?" Ilona enquired.

The Colonel hesitated and she knew that he was considering how much he should tell her.

"Has he . . . changed his mind about the . . . wedding?" she asked.

It was quite on the cards that her father would do so, regardless of the consequences.

"Not exactly," Colonel Ceáky replied. "But His Majesty is, as you might have expected, extremely angry at having been forced to give his consent to it."

"He must realise there is no alternative."

"I am sure it is right that I should tell Your Royal Highness," Colonel Ceáky said, "that the Prime Minister and Prince Aladár called here this morning and asked to see you."

"The Prince?" Ilona exclaimed.

"It was to be expected that he should call," Colonel Ceáky answered.

"I was not told of his arrival."

"No, His Majesty refused to allow either the Prince or the Prime Minister to see you."

Ilona said nothing and Colonel Ceáky went on:

"I am afraid, Princess, that the message that was given to them was not particularly polite."

"What happened?"

"They asked for Your Royal Highness at the door and were shown into one of the Salons. The officer on duty was a young man who considered it his duty to inform His Majesty of the Prime Minister's arrival."

Ilona drew in her breath. She could understand so well what had happened.

"What was the message my father sent to the Prince?" she asked.

The Colonel hesitated before he replied:

"Her Royal Highness, the Princess Ilona of Dabrozka, has no wish to speak to or see Prince Aladár before she is forced by circumstances to do so."

The Colonel spoke in a low voice, then said quickly:

"I deeply regret that this should have happened."

"I insist on seeing my father," Ilona said.

She felt a surge of rage within herself that her father should have behaved so discourteously, so insultingly, towards the man she was to marry.

Could anything be more unfortunate at this particular moment?

Colonel Ceáky did not argue with her but walked across the room and opened the door into the King's apartments. He returned a few seconds later to say briefly:

"His Majesty will see Your Royal Highness!"

Holding her head high, Ilona walked past him into her father's room.

The King was sitting in an arm-chair, his legs sprawled out in front of him, a glass of brandy in his hand, a half-empty decanter on the table by his chair.

"What do you want?" he asked harshly as Ilona advanced towards him.

Ilona curtseyed dutifully.

"I have been waiting to speak to you all the morning, Papa."

"I have no wish to see you," the King remarked in a surly tone.

"I have been told," Ilona said, "that you dismissed Prince Aladár and the Prime Minister in my name. That was not only extremely offensive, Papa, it was also very unwise!"

"What do you mean—unwise?" the King asked, glowering at her.

"If I am to marry Prince Aladár in an effort to save this country and to create an atmosphere of peace amongst our people, it is extremely unfortunate that he should think of me as rude and uncooperative."

"Are you daring to question my action in this matter?" the King asked.

He put down his glass and rose to his feet as he spoke. He looked very tall and aggressive with his dark eye-brows almost meeting across his forehead.

"We have to create a new spirit in the land, Papa," Ilona answered. "We have to put an end to enmity and hatred and make the Radáks and the Sáros meet in friendship."

The King threw back his head and laughed. It was a sound without mirth and it was also contemptuous.

"Do you really think you can change the feeling in the country? You—a creature of no importance save that you are my daughter, dragged up in obscurity by that sanctimonious mother of yours?"

He spoke so violently that for a moment it was difficult for Ilona to find words with which to answer him.

Because she was silent he laughed again.

"If you imagine this farcical wedding will change anything, you are very much mistaken. I do not believe all that hysterical nonsense about the Russians wishing to take over the country."

His voice was louder as he went on:

"But of one thing I am quite certain—that my people, the Radáks, loathe and detest the Sáros to their very guts, and the sacrifice of a milk-faced virgin on the altar of matrimony will not change their minds!"

"I think you are wrong, Papa," Ilona replied. "I think too that there are many injustices in Dabrozka today that should be changed."

It required a great effort to defy him, but she spoke quietly and her eyes were on his face as she spoke.

Suddenly and so unexpectedly that she was taken completely by surprise, he stepped forward and hit her with his open hand on the side of her face.

The blow made her stagger and fall to her knees on the ground.

"How dare you question my laws and my decrees!" the King shouted. "How dare you answer me back in the same way as your mother did!"

There was a ringing in her ears that for the moment made Ilona feel dizzy. Then she suddenly felt the sharp sting of a whip across her shoulders.

Because it was so unexpected, because she had not realised he had picked up a riding-whip, she screamed. Then as the whip fell again and again on her back she bit her lip until it bled.

The agony of the whip was like a knife cutting into her skin. Then she heard her father say roughly:

"Get out of here and stay out of my sight! When you become a Sáros you will soon learn what I think of you!"

It was difficult to move, almost impossible to get to her feet. Ilona felt as if the room was swimming round her. Then pride came to her aid and her feet carried her towards the door.

As she reached out to touch the handle the door opened and she saw that Colonel Ceáky was outside.

She passed him without a word and, leaving the Ante-Chamber, walked slowly back the way she had come and up the Grand Staircase to her bed-room.

Only when she was alone and had shut herself in did she put up her hand to her cheek and feel as if she must faint from the horror of what she had undergone.

She could hardly believe it possible that her father had struck her as he had done when she was a child! The terror he had evoked then flooded over her now like a dark cloud.

"I hate him! I hate him!" Ilona told herself.

The intensity of her feelings swept away the weakness that threatened to overcome her and the tears of pain that pricked her eyes.

She was determined not to be subservient to him or to acknowledge that his strength had defeated her.

She only vowed that because of the manner in

which he had behaved she would fight him and his injustice to the last breath in her body.

* * *

The bells of a dozen Churches were pealing, and the sound mingled with the cheers of the people and the music of the Bands.

In the short time they had been given to prepare for the wedding, the citizens of Vitózi had worked miracles.

There were arches of flowers and the street-lamps were garlanded with them.

There were flags and bunting hanging from every house and every balcony.

The streets were lined with men, women, and children, all dressed in their colourful costumes and waving handkerchiefs, bunches of flowers, and flags.

It was a day of brilliant sunshine, warm but with a faint breeze.

Ilona, seated beside her father in an open carriage, was aware that to the populace she must look the ideal bride, radiant and happy at the prospect of being married.

The gown that she and Magda had chosen from those she had brought from Paris was a ball-gown of white silk and tulle. It had a long train flowing from the bustle, which when she walked moved behind her like a white-crested wave.

She had thought when she purchased it that perhaps there might be a Ball at the Palace or she would wear it on some public occasion at which she had to make a spectacular appearance.

She never dreamt that it would be her wedding-gown, and yet it was a perfect choice for such an occasion.

Her veil, of shadow lace so fine that it might have been made by fairy spiders, had been worn by the Queens of Dabrozka for centuries.

It did not cover her face, but was held in place by a magnificent diamond tiara fashioned like a wreath of flowers. It was so delicately contrived that each flower was flexible and trembled with every movement Ilona made.

Her mother had often spoken of the Crown Jewels, and when Ilona had been allowed to choose what she would wear for her wedding she had gasped at their magnificence.

She had, however, chosen to wear only the diamond wreath, feeling that anything more would seem ostentatious.

Vaguely at the back of her mind she felt they were more the perquisite of the women Magda described as "a disgrace!"

The gardeners had brought her a bouquet of white flowers and she thought as she held them in her lap that at least they would conceal the trembling of her hands.

It was not only the painful weals on her back that made her feel weak, but also the butterflies she felt fluttering inside her.

Only years of discipline prevented her from clinging feverishly to Magda before she left the Palace.

"God bless you, my little *M'mselle!*" Magda had said with tears running down her cheeks.

It was typical of her father, Ilona thought, that he had decreed that none of the servants at the Palace should be present at the ceremony.

"Could you not persuade Papa that it would give them so much pleasure?" Ilona asked Colonel Ceáky. "Especially those who knew my mother?"

"I said exactly what you asked me to say, Princess," the Colonel replied, "and His Majesty replied that as far as he was concerned it was not a 'peep show'!"

It was difficult, Ilona thought, to control the hatred she felt for her father when with ill-grace he seated himself beside her in the carriage.

He was looking magnificent . . . she could not deny that!

His red tunic, covered with decorations, his plumed hat, which he wore as Commander-in-Chief of the Army, and the Dabrozkan coat, falling from one shoulder, heavily embroidered with gold thread, were all impressive.

The gold sword at his side and the jangling spurs on

his highly polished boots were all part of his magnificence.

Only the scowl on his face and the deep resentment
smouldering in his eyes were a warning to Ilona that
he was like a volcano that might erupt at any moment.

She had prayed before she left the Palace that everything might go off smoothly.

If she was to marry for the sake of Dabrozka a man
she had never seen, then it was important that the
wedding should impress the people as a happy event
and a good augur for the future.

One thing was a relief: there was no question of her
talking to her father on the way to the Cathedral.

There were crowds lining the streets, cheering and
throwing flowers into the carriage, from the moment
they left the gates of the Palace until they reached
the city.

The noise in the Square was almost deafening and
the crowds were thicker there than anywhere else.

Ilona could see a number of *Jahász* and *Csikós* who
tended the herds of cows. They must have come in
from the steppes, and she thought it amazing how
quickly they had learnt about what was taking place
in the Capital.

She was also sure, although it was difficult to be certain, that she could distinguish the people who came
from the Sáros side of the river.

It might have been her imagination, but they looked
more prosperous, better dressed, and happier than did
the Radáks.

There was a Guard of Honour of the King's Regiment outside the Cathedral, and when they entered
the dim solemnity of the great building there was the
sweet fragrance of incense and the gleam of the silver
sanctuary lights.

The religion of the Dabrozkans was Eastern Ortho-
dox.

In Paris Ilona had with her mother attended the
Roman Catholic Services at Nôtre Dame, and she only
hoped that she would not make many mistakes.

The Cathedral was packed, and although she kept
her eyes downcast as she proceeded up the aisle on

her father's arm, she was aware that everyone of importance in the country was represented.

In their best silks and satins, in their bustled gowns and feathered hats, the ladies of Dabrozka were very beautiful, while the men, whatever their age, were dashing and exceedingly handsome.

Slowly the King and Ilona proceeded up the aisle.

Now ahead she could see the Archbishop with his long grey beard, supported by a dozen Priests, while acolytes in their red cassocks and lace-edged surplices were swinging the censers containing incense.

Then she was tinglingly aware that waiting for her at the Chancel steps was the figure of a tall man.

She kept her eyes on the ground in front of her and did not dare to raise her head.

She was to be married to a stranger and she could not look at him, fearing she might become more afraid than she was already.

She felt her fingers tighten on her father's arm, then deliberately she relaxed them.

'I must behave as Mama would have wished me to,' she thought. 'I am doing this for Dabrozka, for the people to whom I belong, so that I may bring them peace.'

The thought was somehow comforting. Now the man she was to marry was standing on her right, and yet still she could not look at him.

The Archbishop began the Service.

Someone took Ilona's bouquet from her and then she and her husband-to-be were kneeling side by side on white satin cushions.

She could feel herself vibrating to his presence and wondered if he was vibrating to hers.

She could see out of the corner of her eyes that he was wearing a white tunic and she knew it was a uniform, although he would not be in any of the Regiments that her father commanded.

Perhaps the Sáros had their own.

She thought how ignorant she was not only of the man she was to marry but also of the part of the country he represented.

She had lost her place in the Service and before she expected it they were actually about to make their wedding-vows.

The man beside her was repeating his after the Archbishop:

"I, Aladár Sebastyen Ladislas, take thee, Ilona Nandina, to be my wedded wife."

He had a deep voice. There was something resonant about it.

He spoke slowly, seriously, and with a positiveness that made him sound sincere.

In contrast, Ilona thought, her own voice sounded weak and helpless.

She felt the Prince's hand take hers to place a narrow gold ring on her third finger.

She had a sudden moment of panic in case it was too small, and thought that if it was, the congregation would take it as a bad omen.

The Dabrozkans were very superstitious about such things.

But the ring fitted perfectly, and the manner in which he held her hand as the Archbishop joined them together was as firm and positive as his voice.

"I now pronounce that you be man and wife together," the Archbishop intoned above their heads.

For the first time Ilona raised her eyes to look at the man whose wife she had become.

For a moment she stared at him incredulously and thought she must be dreaming.

Then she realised that, far from marrying someone unknown to her and whom she had never seen, she had in fact not only seen Prince Aladár before but he had actually kissed her lips!

His blue eyes regarded her quizzically. Then with her heart thumping in her breast, she forced herself to attend to the rest of the Service.

When it was over, Ilona turned to curtsey to the King while the Prince bowed his head ceremoniously.

But as they did so her father rose from the carved seat on which he had been sitting during the Service and walked ahead of them down the aisle.

It was an unprecedented action, but Ilona knew that he did so to show not only the congregation but also her husband that he was the Monarch!

He was the most important person present, even at the marriage of his daughter!

The Prince had offered Ilona his arm and she took it, moving at his side down the aisle behind her father, determined that there should be no expression on her face save one of happiness.

She forced a smile to her lips, and she bowed to the people on the left side of the aisle, knowing that they were finding it difficult, having curtseyed to the King, to curtsey again so quickly to herself and to her husband.

The King had already left in his carriage before they reached theirs.

It was not the same vehicle in which she had arrived at the Cathedral. It was also open, but now the hood and the high seat on which the coachman was seated were decorated with white flowers.

There were white plumes on the horses' heads and their harness was of white, the accoutrements of gold.

It was so pretty and so ornamented that as Ilona stepped into it she knew that this carriage had not come from her father's stables but must in fact belong to the Prince.

There had been cheers when she entered the Capital, but it was nothing compared to the enthusiasm with which the crowds greeted them as Ilona and Prince Aladár left the Cathedral for the Palace.

There seemed, too, to be more flowers, more waving handkerchiefs, more flags, and a more genuine welcome in the voices of those who acclaimed them.

She glanced shyly at the Prince but saw that he was intent on waving to the people on his side of the carriage, and because she knew it was expected of her she concentrated on those on her left.

There were four horses pulling the lightweight vehicle and it did not take them long to cover the distance from the city and climb the steep hill up to the Palace itself.

Behind them was a long line of carriages bringing

all the dignitaries, nobles, landlords, and clergy of Dabrozka to the Reception.

The court-yard of the Palace was full of soldiers and as the carriage drew up outside the door the Prince said:

"I think it is intended that we should inspect the Guard of Honour!"

"Yes, of course," Ilona answered.

She looked at him and now there was no mistaking the amused expression in his eyes and the smile on his lips.

"We have met before," he said.

Because she thought he was remembering that he had kissed her, the blood rose in her cheeks and her eye-lashes fluttered, then lay very dark against her white skin.

She had the feeling that he was laughing at her embarrassment.

Then they were walking down the lines of the Guard of Honour, the Prince stopping occasionally to speak to one of the soldiers. Ilona saw that Major Kassa was the Officer in Charge, and told him how smart the troops were, knowing that it would please him.

By the time they reached the Throne-Room, where the Reception was to be held, the mirrors were reflecting the colourful and distinguished guests, and the very chandeliers seemed to tinkle with the excited chatter of their voices.

There was a six-tiered cake in front of the dais on which stood the Thrones, and Ilona wondered how the Chefs of the Palace had managed to complete so elaborate a cake so quickly.

She thought that she must remember to thank them and also to be quite sure that Magda had a piece.

But it was almost impossible to think of anything except the people crowding round her offering their congratulations.

Many of them spoke of her mother and how much she had been missed; but some stared at her critically and she was quite certain that they came from Sáros land, on the other side of the river.

The Reception seemed to go on interminably and Ilona was glad when Colonel Ceáky brought her a sandwich to eat and a glass of champagne.

"We had hoped that His Majesty would propose the health of the bride and bridegroom," the Colonel said in a low voice that only she could hear, "but he seems to have disappeared!"

"Perhaps it would be best to ask the Prime Minister to do so," Ilona answered.

She had the feeling that it would be unwise to press her father to take an active part in the celebrations.

Colonel Ceáky nodded and a moment later the Prime Minister stepped onto the dais in front of the Thrones.

He held a glass of champagne in his hand.

"Your Majesty, Your Royal Highness, Your Highness, my Lords, Ladies and Gentlemen," he began. "This is a very happy day in the history of Dabrozka. I believe that from this moment the problems and the difficulties that have been ours for the past few years will be swept away.

"There will be no more divisions, no more partitions, neither in our country nor in our hearts. Prince Aladár and his beautiful wife will bring a new spirit to the land we love."

He paused to say impressively:

"May we, each of us, make our contribution, not only in words and actions but also with our very hearts and souls."

The Prime Minister spoke with such sincerity that it was very moving.

Then he raised his glass to say:

"I propose the toast of the bride and bridegroom, God give them many years of happiness together and bring us what we need so greatly—peace!"

There was a cry of:

"The bride and bridegroom!"

Glasses were raised and the toast was drunk.

Taking Ilona by the hand, the Prince stepped onto the dais.

"I wish to thank the Prime Minister on behalf of my wife and myself and assure him that we dedicate ourselves to the service of Dabrozka. There will be no more enmity between the Radáks and Sáros and the divisions that have kept us apart for so long no longer exist.

"I believe that with your help we can create a new country, as we begin a new family life that we hope will set an example of peace and prosperity to generations of future Dabrozkans.'"

Everybody clapped and a number of men cheered as the Prince turned to Ilona and raised her hand to his lips.

She felt his mouth hard and insistent on her soft skin and felt a little tremor go through her.

Then as she looked up at him, feeling that she should say something but not certain what it should be, there was a voice behind her.

"His Majesty wishes to speak to Your Royal Highness and to you, Sir!"

It was one of her father's Aides-de-Camp and Ilona fancied there was something hostile in his tone.

She glanced at him apprehensively, but he walked ahead, leading them through an adjacent door into one of the Ante-Chambers that adjoined the Hall of Mirrors.

The King was waiting alone for them and one look at the expression on his face made Ilona's heart feel as if it had stopped beating.

He was glowering in the same way he had glowered at her yesterday. As the door closed behind them he said harshly to the Prince:

"I heard what you said!"

"I hope it pleased you, Sire."

"Pleased me?" the King ejaculated. "Did you think it would please me that you should speak as if you intend to sit on my Throne and breed children who will usurp my position?"

"I have no wish to usurp your position, Sire," the Prince replied. "But I understood that my wife was to be your heir and when the time comes to reign over Dabrozka . . ."

"*When* the time comes!" the King said. "And by that time—you upstart—you will be dead."

Ilona felt the Prince stiffen beside her, but before he could speak the King went on, working himself into one of his tyrannical rages as he shouted:

"I understand only too well what is in your crafty mind. You think that if I will accept you I will accept your children! You are mistaken! You will not touch my daughter, and if you dare to do so I will kill you with my bare hands!"

He pointed his finger derisively as he yelled:

"You are nothing but a common bandit! The so-called Princes of Sáros are no better than the rebellious peasants over whom they rule!

"If you want a woman, then take one from among the dirty gypsies you have encouraged to break my laws: and who are undoubtedly the right companions for a man of your sort! Maybe your father was a gypsy, if the truth be known."

The King was crimson in the face and spitting with rage as he said:

"I have been forced—yes, forced—to give you my daughter in marriage. But make no mistake, it is only a farce, a charade to deceive the Russians! It is not an invitation for you to exercise your filthy lust or to treat her as if she were not your superior by birth and breeding."

Shaking his fist now, he shouted:

"She loathes you, as I do, and to her you are nothing but a lackey! If I had my way, I would have you whipped from this Palace and hanged as the prisoners you released the other night will be hanged as soon as they are caught!"

Ilona stood mesmerised into immobility by her father's tirade.

She felt as if his grotesquely contorted face and his snarling voice hypnotised her so that she could not move and could not even protest what he was saying.

Then she felt the Prince take her arm and move her towards the door that led not into the Hall of Mirrors but into the corridor.

As they reached it and the King realised what they were about, he shouted:

"Come back! I have not finished with you, yet, Sáros. I have more to say—more I wish you to hear!"

The Prince turned and bowed his head correctly. As if he had told her to do so, Ilona curtseyed. Then he opened the door and they were in the passage.

He drew her towards the Great Hall and because she thought he did not know the way she tried to turn left to the Throne-Room.

"We are leaving!"

The Prince's voice was quite expressionless, but when she looked at his face she saw that his eyes were hard and his chin was square-set.

She could feel the waves of anger emanating from him, and her heart, which seemed to have stood still during her father's outburst, began to beat apprehensively.

She wanted to protest, to suggest they should go back and at least explain to the Prime Minister what had happened.

Then she thought that it was quite unnecessary.

He would doubtless learn from the King himself what had happened; but in any case it would not be hard for him to guess the reason for their precipitate departure.

They reached the Hall and the servants on duty looked at them in surprise.

"My carriage!" the Prince ordered.

The Major-Domo hurried through the open door and descended the steps to call up the flower-decorated carriage, which was waiting in the shade. The coachmen had obviously not expected to be required for some time.

Hastily it was driven to the bottom of the steps, and as if she were an automaton with no will of her own Ilona stepped into it. The Prince sat down beside her.

There were no guests to see them go, no cries of good luck, no flower-petals or rice.

The sentries came to attention, the coachmen whipped up the horses, and they started down the drive.

Chapter Four

Ilona tried to apologise to the Prince but it was impossible to find words.

She was stunned at her father's behaviour and numb to the point where her brain would not work.

She felt just as helpless and subservient as she had when he had whipped her, and all she could think of for the moment was that her back was hurting her almost intolerably.

"I must speak to the Prince—I must say how sorry I am," she told herself, but even as her lips opened to form the words, the carriage reached the Palace gates.

There were cheers and cries from the crowds congregated outside, waving from the roadside, shouting from the trees up which they had climbed.

Automatically Ilona began to bow and wave her hand and she knew that it would be impossible to make herself heard by the Prince above the noise.

The road was lined with people all the way to Vitózi, and when they reached the bridge over the river it was almost impossible for the horses to pass through the crowds on either side of it.

Cries of "Good luck!" and "Good wishes!" accompanied the flowers that were thrown into the carriage, and there were showers of rose-petals and rice, which was quite painful when it struck Ilona's face.

But there was no doubt of the general goodwill and excitement, and on the other side of the river the enthusiasm rose to a crescendo.

Now they were on Sáros land and Ilona realised it

had not been her imagination that the citizens here looked more prosperous and certainly happier.

There was a Square not far from the bridge and in the centre of it was a statue.

It was garlanded with flowers and Ilona could see by the inscription on its base that it had been erected to a Prince of Sáros.

Here the crowds surged round the carriage and it was impossible for the horses to move.

"Speech! Speech!"

The cry was taken up first by one group and then another, until the hundreds of people in the Square were all intoning the same words.

The Prince rose to his feet in the carriage. Then as if he remembered that the women would wish to see Ilona also, he offered her his hand to assist her to her feet.

She knew that her fingers were trembling as she placed them in his.

She rose to stand beside him and there was a sudden expectant hush over the crowd as they realised he was about to address them.

He said almost the same words that he had spoken in the Throne-Room, except that he finished by saying:

"Peace is possible only with your help and your co-operation. There must be no more fighting amongst ourselves. We are threatened by an enemy from outside this country and only if we are united as one people can we survive!"

"He loves Dabrozka," Ilona told herself.

For the first time, she wondered if the idea of uniting the country by their marriage had perhaps come from him.

The horses moved on but there was still no question of their having any kind of conversation with each other.

The roads were already lined with people and many of those who had been in the city accompanied them, running beside the carriage or behind it, still shouting and cheering even when they climbed the steep hill that led to Sáros Castle.

Ilona had her first glimpse of it through the blossom-laden acacia-trees and saw that it was far more beautiful than she had expected it to be.

There was a high tower on one side, and the building was decorated with small turrets, arched doorways, and ornamental stone carvings, which made it seem like a Castle in a fairy-tale.

There were no walls to enclose it and make it seem a fortification like the Palace.

Instead, there were shrubberies of rhododendrons and azaleas, crimson, yellow, and white, and the purple of the Judas-trees contrasted strikingly with the green leaves of the myrtle and the silver-grey of the olive.

The soldiers lined up outside the Castle were wearing uniforms very different from those worn by the King's soldiers, and Ilona realised that the Prince had his own Army.

It explained why her father had not attacked the Sáros land, which he might have done if there had been no troops there to oppose him.

'No wonder Papa hates the Sáros!' she thought.

The carriage drew up outside the Castle door, and as soon as Ilona alighted the Prince presented to her his household staff and the officers in charge of the troops.

Both the men and the women seemed to be much younger than those Ilona had met at the Palace.

It was pleasing to be aware that the officers, extremely handsome in their smart uniforms, had an unmistakable gleam of admiration in their eyes when they were presented to her.

They walked into the Castle and Ilona saw that it was not at all awe-inspiring or overpowering like the Palace.

There were many heads of wild animals on the walls, besides portraits of beautiful women and handsome men who she knew must be the Prince's ancestors.

She had only a quick glance at these before she raised her eyes to her husband, wondering apprehensively if he was still as angry as he had been when they left the Palace.

"I am sure," he said quietly in a voice that was quite expressionless, "that you would like to rest. The Housekeeper will show you the way to your apartments."

Ilona hesitated.

She wanted to ask him if they could be alone for a few minutes, but she knew that anything she said would be overheard and she felt that it would be embarrassing.

She curtseyed and then, with the train of her gown falling gracefully behind her, walked up the staircase.

Only as she reached the top, where the Housekeeper was waiting, did she hear laughter and voices from below and realise that the Prince was surrounded by his officers, who were congratulating him.

The Housekeeper, carrying a large bunch of keys dangling from her waist to show her status, welcomed Ilona to the Castle, and led her to a large room where three windows overlooked the valley.

"This, Your Royal Highness," she said, "is the room used by all the Princesses of Sáros for many centuries, and of course His Highness's apartments are next door."

It was a beautiful room, and the furniture was, Ilona knew, of Dabrozkan craftsmanship.

The wood, cut from special trees in the forests, was inlaid with other woods, forming patterns of flowers and birds and sometimes animals.

The posts of the large bed were exquisitely carved and painted, for there was no-one to equal the Dabrozkan carvers and their work made every Church and every important building a riot of beauty and colour.

There were fat cupids flying over towards the ceiling, holding aloft the Sáros Coronet, and the alpine flowers of the valley were depicted in their glorious blues, pinks, yellows, and greens.

She could also see carvings of the fox, the wild cat, the lizard, and the bearded eagle, besides the leaping salmon that filled the waters of the lakes.

"I have never seen anything so lovely!" Ilona exclaimed.

The Housekeeper looked pleased.

"It is very old, Your Royal Highness, but like most things in the Castle, it was made and is tended by loving hands."

"That is what makes a home," Ilona said involuntarily.

"That is true, Your Royal Highness, and we are all praying that you will be very happy here."

"I . . . want to be," Ilona said almost beneath her breath.

When Magda joined her there was the unpacking to do not only in the bed-room but also in the Sitting-Room that opened off it.

The Prince had suggested to Ilona that she should rest, but although she felt tired and her back was stiff and aching from the whipping her father had given her the previous day, she refused to lie down.

Instead she moved from room to room, often going to the windows to look out over the valley at the Palace on the far side of it.

She wondered what her father had done after they had left.

She was afraid that he might have gone into the Throne-Room and berated or insulted the guests.

Even to think of the manner in which he had spoken to the Prince made her feel physically sick.

"How could any man," she asked, "forgive such an insult?"

She realised that if any other Dabrozkan had been spoken to in such terms, he would have felt that his honour could only be avenged in blood.

But instead they had come away without the Prince saying one word in reply.

His self-control was admirable, but she was well aware that it constituted a disastrous start to her marriage.

She wondered if he believed that she was in league with her father against him.

Could anything have been more unfortunate than

his being sent away from the Palace yesterday morning?

If only she had known he was there . . . if only she could have met him, as he had intended, before the wedding.

Then she remembered how he had kissed her in the woods and the mocking note in his voice when he had said:

"Go home, pretty lady, and flirt with your beaux."

What had he meant by that?

Had he thought that because she was unaccompanied she was someone of no importance, or perhaps —a more frightening idea—that she was like the ladies in Paris who rode or drove alone in the Bois to show off their attractions?

"Surely he could not . . . think that?" Ilona asked herself in horror.

Then common sense told her that the mere fact that he had kissed her in that cavalier manner made it seem very probable.

She felt as if she were caught in the centre of some terrible whirlpool and that everything she did, every move she made, sucked her deeper and deeper into the vortex from which there was no escape.

"I will explain," she told herself bravely. "When we meet this evening, I will explain everything to him from the very beginning."

She was talking to Magda about two hours later when there was a knock on the door of the Sitting-Room.

Magda went to open it.

She spoke for a moment to whoever was outside, then returned to Ilona's side to day:

"There is a gentleman, *M'mselle*, who says he is His Highness's Secretary and desires to speak to you."

"Ask him to come in," Ilona said, getting to her feet.

It was a relief that anyone wished to speak to her.

She had begun to think that she had been forgotten.

An elderly man with grey hair came into the room, bowed respectfully, and said:

"His Highness has asked me to supply you, Ma'am, with a list of your engagements for tomorrow, so that you should be prepared for them, and to inform you that there will be a dinner-party tonight, at which you will meet His Highness's relatives who live in the vicinity."

"Thank you," Ilona replied. "May I know your name?"

"It is Duzsa, Ma'am. Count Duzsa."

"And you are Secretary to my husband?"

Count Duzsa smiled.

"That is one of my jobs, Ma'am. I am in fact Comptroller, Supervisor of the Castle, and general factotum!"

Ilona gave a little laugh.

"I can see you are very busy!"

"Not too busy to be of service to you, Ma'am, whenever you may require me."

"Thank you, Count. I hope you will help me not to make too many mistakes. As I expect you know, I have not been in Dabrozka for many years and am very out of touch with all the problems that have arisen recently."

"We are all praying, Ma'am, that they will now disappear."

"I hope so."

Count Duzsa would have left the room, but as he reached the door Ilona gave a little cry.

"Please . . . please do not go," she pleaded. "Tell me about my husband's relatives and who I shall be meeting this evening. As you will appreciate, it is all rather alarming for me."

She thought that there was a kindness and an understanding in the elderly man's eyes that had not been there before.

"Of course," he replied. "I have a list of who will be here at dinner, and I will try to explain not only who they are but also the very interwoven and complex relationships of the Sáros."

He sat down at Ilona's invitation and they talked for nearly an hour.

She learnt for the first time that the Princes of

Sáros were actually a far older family than were the Radáks.

But because they were not in the least ambitious and had been content to live the lives of country gentlemen, or travel abroad, the head of the Radáks had without opposition become the reigning Monarch.

There were, the Count explained, an enormous number of Sáros, many of whom were married or related to the Crowned Heads of Europe, and yet were still content to play a comparatively minor role in the management of their own country.

What she learnt made it even worse, Ilona thought, when she remembered the manner in which her father had insulted the Prince.

After Count Duzsa had left her she told herself over and over again that she must apologise to the Prince and beg him to forget what her father had said.

"This is a happy place, *M'mselle*," Magda said as she helped Ilona into her evening-gown.

"Why do you say that?"

"I know when people are happy," Magda replied, "and it is not just because there has been a wedding in the Castle today. Everyone is smiling and singing!"

"I want to hear them sing," Ilona murmured.

She moved across the beautiful bed-room to look at herself in the long mirror, which was framed with carved cupids, painted and gilded.

The gown she had chosen tonight was white, which she felt was correct for a bride, but there was a glimmer of silver beneath the gauze of which it was made.

There were also bunches of white flowers among the draperies, caught with silver ribbons and glittering with diamanté.

It was a gown such as only Paris could design, and as she fastened the glittering rose-buds in Ilona's red hair, which fell from the back of her head in small curls, Magda cried:

"You look lovely, *M'mselle*. I only wish your dear mother could see you now."

"Perhaps she . . . can," Ilona replied.

The thought of her mother was always with her.

A little earlier when she was taking her bath Magda

had given a shrill cry as for the first time she saw the deep purple weals on her back, which had been left by her father's whip.

"M'mselle, what has happened? Who can have done this to you?" she asked.

Ilona had stepped quickly from the bath and wrapped a large towel round her.

"I had a fall out riding, Magda," she replied. "It is not important. I did not hurt myself."

They both knew it was a lie: Magda was well aware whose whip had marked Ilona's white skin, and that she was ruled by the same pride that prevented the Queen from complaining.

Magda understood, and she said:

"Of course, M'mselle, but tonight when you undress I will treat it with some cream that will help to make the bruises fade quickly."

'Whatever happens now, however difficult it may be,' Ilona thought to herself irrepressibly, 'I am free of Papa and he will no longer be able to beat me.'

As if the very idea gave her a feeling of freedom, she walked down the staircase to dinner with a smile on her lips.

She knew she looked attractive and that, however angry the Prince might be, he would not be ashamed to introduce her to his relatives.

She remembered the feeling of his lips on hers and she felt a little tremor of excitement go through her as she thought that perhaps tonight, after everyone had left, he would kiss her again.

The servants showed Ilona into a big Salon that was fragrant with the scent of the flowers that stood on every table.

At the far end of the room, about twenty people were talking and laughing.

In the centre of them she could see the Prince, looking, she thought, smarter and more handsome than ever in his evening-clothes.

He walked towards her and she looked up at him, hoping he would understand a little of what she was feeling when he met her eyes.

Although he raised her hand perfunctorily to his lips

he did not look at her directly, but led her forward to introduce her to the assembled company.

To Ilona, dinner was a very gay and amusing meal.

She had never before attended a big dinner-party or eaten off gold plates, and certainly she had never before been tempted by such delicious dishes, which succeeded one another until it was impossible to eat any more.

The Prince's relatives not only looked attractive, they were also charming, gay, and witty.

It was not the quiet, erudite conversation of her mother's elderly friends to which Ilona now listened, but the sparkling repartee of people with agile minds who could throw the conversational ball backwards and forwards between them as if playing an intriguing game.

Ilona was not able to take part in much of what was being said, but for the first time in her life she received fulsome but nevertheless sincere compliments both from the ladies and the gentlemen.

The dining-table was a long one.

While she sat at one end, with the Prince's uncle on one side and a young and extremely handsome cousin on the other, the Prince was at the far end.

It was difficult to see him clearly because of the gold candelabra, the great bowls of peaches and grapes, and the intricately arranged table-decorations, which were all white.

When the meal was finished the ladies moved back into the Salon and soon the gentlemen joined them. Several of the older members of the family sat down to play cards.

The rest—and they were mostly the Prince's younger relatives—gathered round Ilona and one of them said to the Prince:

"This is a rather dull evening, I should have thought, for someone as young and beautiful as your bride."

"I am afraid my wife will find Dabrozka very dull and staid after the gaieties and frivolities of France," the Prince replied coldly.

Ilona looked at him in surprise.

Did he really think she had been able to enjoy such amusements in Paris?

Then she told herself that he was just as ignorant of her previous life as she was of his.

'There is so much we have to tell each other,' she thought with a little sigh.

The party did not continue for very long.

The older people wished to return home, and although it was obvious that the others would have liked to linger, they tactfully assumed that the bride and bridegroom would wish to be alone.

Without ceremony Ilona and the Prince said good-bye to their guests in the Hall, and his aunt, an elderly woman who had once been a great beauty, expressed the feelings of the rest as she said to Ilona:

"We are so happy, my dear, to welcome you as one of the family. You are very lovely and I feel that you and Aladár will make each other happy."

She kissed Ilona as she spoke, and one of the Prince's cousins when he kissed her hand said:

"I only wish I had met you first. Aladár always did have all the luck!"

Laughing and still paying Ilona compliments, they drove away.

As the servants shut the big door behind them, Ilona realised that the Prince was waiting for her to go upstairs.

He did not speak, and feeling shy now that they were alone, she merely did as he expected, moving up the staircase with her hand on the bannister.

Magda was waiting for her in the big bed-room. There were candelabra lit on either side of the cupid-decorated bed and large thick candles in gold stands to light the room.

One of Ilona's new and entrancing night-gowns, which she had bought in Paris, was lying over a velvet-covered chair.

She undressed almost in silence. As she got into bed, she was rehearsing in her mind what she could say to the Prince when he came to her.

"Good-night, my little *M'mselle*," Magda said from the doorway. "God bless you."

"Good-night Magda."

The door shut behind the old maid and Ilona was alone.

She lay back against the pillows, realising that her heart was beating tumultuously and her mouth was dry.

'I am frightened,' she thought.

She was not certain whether it was the Prince of whom she was afraid or the apology she had to make to him.

It was nearly half an hour later when she heard him speaking to someone.

She thought it must be a servant on duty or perhaps one of the nightwatchmen who, Magda had told her, patrolled the Castle at night.

There were also soldiers on duty. Ilona as she lay in bed had heard them marching outside in the courtyard, and she realised that the Prince, having an Army of his own, was guarded in the same manner as her father was.

There will always be the chance, Ilona thought, that the enemy who had infiltrated the country might try to attack the Prince.

She felt herself shiver a little at the idea, then told herself that she must never under any circumstance let anyone know that she was afraid of the Russians.

The door opened and her heart gave an apprehensive leap as the Prince came into the room.

He looked tall and very dignified in a long brocade robe that reached to the ground.

The door was some distance from the bed and Ilona waited for him to walk towards her. Now that the moment was upon her, she tried desperately to think how she should frame the apology she knew she must make.

Then to her astonishment the Prince walked only a little way into the room and sat down in one of the velvet-covered arm-chairs.

He arranged his robe, leant back against a satin cushion, and opening a book he was carrying in his hand began to read.

Ilona stared at him wide-eyed in amazement.

It flashed through her mind that perhaps he held a Bible or a prayer-book in his hands.

Was this a Dabrozkan custom of which she was not aware?

The Prince was reading with apparent interest.

He turned over the page, and watching him Ilona felt that he was in fact completely concentrating on his book.

Her eyes were on his face, which was half in profile, and she thought that it would be impossible to imagine that any man could be better-looking!

His square forehead and thick dark hair, his straight aristocratic nose, and the deep-set blue eyes, which she knew could twinkle mockingly, made her think of a Greek god.

She felt as though his very features were engraved in her mind as she waited—and went on waiting!

'I must speak to him,' Ilona thought. 'I must ask him what he is doing.'

Then she realised that she did not know how to address him.

Although he was her husband, she found it almost impossible to call him "Aladár" before they got to know each other, and how could she say "Prince," or "Your Highness"?

It would seem ridiculous!

'Perhaps when he reaches the end of this page,' she thought, 'he will speak to me.'

But the Prince turned the page and yet another, while Ilona lay in the shadows of the silk curtains, her red hair falling over her shoulders, her eyes very green in the candlelight.

Finally the Prince closed his book.

Ilona drew in her breath.

Now at last he would come to her and she would be able to say all she wished to.

But the Prince rose to his feet and without even one glance at Ilona he walked to the door. It closed quietly behind him.

As if released from the intolerable tension she had been suffering, Ilona sat up in bed.

As she did so she saw that it was an hour—exactly

an hour—since the Prince had come to her room, and putting her hands up to her face she understood exactly what he had intended.

There were always eyes to see and ears to hear, whether it was in a Palace, a Castle, or a house.

If the Prince had ignored his bride on the first night of their marriage, it would undoubtedly have been noticed and reported by someone. Such a tit-bit of gossip would have been whispered from mouth to mouth.

Then the whole of Dabrozka would have been aware that the marriage was, as the King had said, only "a farce and a charade" to deceive the Russians.

Instead, as far as the world was concerned, the Prince had done his duty!

He had gone to his wife's bed-room and it would be believed that he had made love to her and they were man and wife not only in name but in actual fact.

The humiliation of it made Ilona throw herself down again on the bed, but this time her face was hidden in the pillow.

He did not want her!

She had been forced upon him by circumstances, and while once he had kissed her because he thought her lovely, he was completely indifferent to her charms now that she was his wife.

She knew little about men and less about love.

Yet she had always heard that if a woman was attractive, men desired her, even though what they felt was not love, not the real love a woman sought in marriage.

But as far as the Prince was concerned she did not even interest him to the point where he wished to kiss her lips or even talk to her.

Whatever her father had said, Ilona thought, however rude and offensive he had been, surely the Prince was not so angry as to loathe her, as her father's daughter, as he loathed the King?

"He must not feel like that—he must not!" Ilona told herself piteously. "I must make him see that I am different. . . . I must explain to him!"

But even as she spoke the words into her pillow she thought despairingly that it might be impossible.

* * *

Ilona walked to the window and looked out at the sunshine on the valley below.

Every day it seemed to her that the view was more breath-taking, the snow-peaked mountains more exquisite against the blue sky, the river winding its way into the green distance more alluring, and every day she grew more miserable.

"Which gown do you wish to wear today, *M'mselle?*" asked Magda, behind her.

"It does not matter," Ilona replied dully.

For four days, she reflected, she had taken trouble over her appearance, tried to look beautiful, attempted to arouse a response of some sort from her husband, only to have failed!

For four days she had been the wife of the Prince, and never once had he spoken to her when they were alone or addressed her in public without a cold note in his voice that told her what he was feeling.

They were always surrounded by people.

Every day they had visited one of the towns in Dabrozka to be welcomed officially by the Burgomaster and the other dignitaries in the area, and to receive presentations and gifts and hear speeches.

Everywhere they were acclaimed in the same enthusiastic manner that had characterised their wedding.

Ilona had learnt a lot about the Prince on these expeditions.

She realised not only his popularity, but also the fact that he had such authority in the country owing to his remarkable personality.

The people looked on him with respect and admiration, and they also trusted him and believed what he told them.

Their visits to the towns, Ilona knew, were not only to receive the goodwill of the inhabitants but also to give them courage and a new hope for the future.

Despite the penal taxation, despite the cruel and unjust laws that her father had passed, Ilona was aware that the Prince aroused in them a sense of patriotism.

Without being in the least disloyal to the reigning Monarch, he contrived to make the people believe that a golden future lay ahead.

'But how will it ever be accomplished while Papa lives?' Ilona wondered sometimes.

She found herself carried away as everyone else was by the Prince's deep voice and by the sincerity with which he spoke.

His love of Dabrozka inspired those who listened to him to the point where Ilona sometimes thought they almost worshipped him.

But while ordinarily she would have loved the drives from Vitózi to the other towns, the beauty of the countryside, the mountains towering above them, and the spontaneous welcome they received even in the smallest hamlets, they were never alone.

Facing them in the open carriage were usually two young officers who acted as the Prince's Aides-de-Camp. They found it difficult, Ilona realised, to look anywhere but at her face.

The Prince talked to them, laughing and joking, as if he were their equal rather than their Commanding Officer, just as he treated everyone he met with a comradeship that swept away stiffness and protocol and made even the most pompous Mayoral Banquet an occasion of gaiety and laughter.

He was also delightfully unpredictable.

He would do unexpected things, like picking up a small boy and letting him ride with them in the carriage.

Or he would toast the most unimportant official's wife at a Banquet, making her the most envied woman in the whole gathering.

He listened to stories of complaints and tragedies, commiserated with bereaved wives, congratulated young soldiers, and admired the herds of sheep and cattle that were the pride of every Dabrozkan farmer.

He was indefatigable!

Often as they drove homewards after a long day he would sing the peasant songs that Ilona remembered from her childhood, his Aides-de-Camp joining in while Ilona was quite certain that the coachmen on the box were singing beneath their breath.

It was only when everyone had left the Castle and the dinner guests who arrived every night had departed that the Prince turned from a warm, gay, laughing young man into an icicle of coldness and repression.

Every night he came to Ilona's room, bringing his book, to seat himself in the same chair, and he always stayed exactly one hour before he rose to leave.

She had been too shy and too humiliated to speak to him until last night.

Then when he had been there a long time, when she could bear it no longer, she said aloud:

"Aladár!"

She was no nervous that after she had spoken she thought it was impossible for him to have heard her because her voice seemed to have died in her throat.

With a superhuman effort she spoke again.

"Aladár!"

This time he heard her.

He shut his book and she thought with a sudden quickening of her senses that at last she would get some response from him.

Instead, he had gone from the room as he had done on the previous nights, only this time he was half an hour earlier in retiring.

She had given a cry of sheer misery and spent the rest of the night tossing and turning and asking herself how long it could continue.

She knew only too well that the next day would be like yesterday and the day before that.

They would visit the same sort of people, go through the same motions, say the same things. Aladár would inspire them as he had done the others, and they would drive home to entertain another large dinnerparty.

If only they had been happy with each other, Ilona thought, every moment would have been an excitement and a delight because they were doing something together that was really worthwhile.

It was what she had wanted in life, what her mother would have wanted for her.

But now, although she was doing her duty, it was difficult and miserable, because every moment of the day she was conscious of the Prince's feelings towards her.

It seemed to Ilona, when she went downstairs the next morning to find the carriage waiting as usual to carry them to some town that was many miles away, that the Prince's coldness seemed even more marked than it had been at any time since they were married.

He addressed her only when it was unavoidable, and the note in his voice was like an icy wind blowing from the snows above them.

He never looked at her directly and when circumstances forced him to touch her she felt almost as if his fingers were frozen and there was no warmth in them.

"He hates me!" she told herself.

This afternoon, however, the Prince did not start the singing and seemed unusually silent.

The Aides-de-Camp made some remarks to him, but he answered them in monosyllables and Ilona thought miserably that even they must be aware sooner or later that there was something wrong.

After only four days of marriage, she told herself, there was an invisible barrier between herself and the Prince that was more effective than iron and steel could ever be.

She was thankful when at last the Castle was in sight.

Then unexpectedly, the Prince's spirits seemed to revive and he talked more animatedly than he had during the whole journey.

As they stepped into the Hall, Count Duzsa was there to meet them and Ilona was genuinely glad to see him.

She had grown to like and rely on the Count since she had been at the Castle.

He told her so many things she wanted to know. He gave her a short biography of every guest she met at the dinner-parties and also told her many legends and stories about the towns they visited.

"You are quite right, Count," Ilona said as she reached his side, "the place we visited today looked exactly like a falcon's nest!"

"I thought you would see the similarity, Ma'am," he replied.

"And the people were very musical."

"A different sort of music from what you will hear this evening!"

"This evening?" Ilona questioned.

"I thought His Highness would have told you," he said, looking towards Prince Aladár, who had followed Ilona into the Hall.

"Told me what?" Ilona asked.

"That the gypsies are to be your hosts."

The Count saw the surprise in Ilona's face and explained:

"There are a great number of gypsies in Sáros, as I know you are well aware, and they are deeply grateful to the Prince for allowing them to stay on his land and for protecting them."

"From the King?" Ilona asked.

"His Majesty would have sent the Army against them, had it not been for the Prince's intervention!"

The Count looked at the Prince and asked:

"Is that not true, Sir?"

"My wife may dislike the gypsies as much as her father does," the Prince replied coldly, "in which case she will not be interested in hearing of their gratitude. If she does not wish to be present tonight, I can easily make excuses for her absence."

He was speaking, Ilona thought, as if she were not there, and she found that it made her angry.

"I should be delighted to attend the gypsies' party," she said to the Count, "and as I am certain it would be expected for us to make them some small gift, perhaps you would be kind enough to choose something appropriate to the occasion."

She turned towards the stairs as she spoke, and with almost a flounce of her skirts she walked away, with her head held high.

'I am growing very tired,' she thought to herself, 'of

the Prince's high-handed manner! Sooner or later I will force him to talk to me!'

As she walked up the stairs, she continued to herself:

'It is impossible to do so when I am in bed. The only way will be for me to ask him to come to my Sitting-Room, or perhaps I could go to his.'

She tried to sound to herself defiant and determined.

But something weak and helpless inside her made her feel that the Prince was so overpowering and so self-confident that whatever she did would merely make her look foolish in his eyes.

Supposing he asked her what, if she was not satisfied with the way he was treating her, she had expected?

It would be impossible for her to tell him what she really wanted without laying herself open to the obvious retort that he did not find her attractive.

'That is the whole truth,' Ilona thought, 'I do not attract him, and nothing I can say or do will make any difference!'

She expected to endure a miserable evening of cold indifference from the Prince and a pretence on her part of being interested in everybody else but him.

She was finding it more and more difficult to play that part, but actually that night she did not have to pretend.

The gypsies had congregated just outside the gardens of the Castle and because it was a warm evening with a sky filled with a multitude of stars, the Prince and Ilona walked from the Castle to where the gypsies were waiting for them.

Servants accompanied them with lighted torches, and when they were met by the gypsy Chief, or *Voivode*, Ilona found that they were the only guests, the only people present who were not of gypsy blood.

Her memories of the gypsies were always of small ragged bands moving about the countryside, attending the fairs where they sold their wares, told fortunes, or collected crowds round their performing animals.

But she had never met the gypsies as a tribe and led by their *Voivode*.

She had heard that many of them wielded great power amongst their people, but even so she had not expected to see one so elaborately dressed or wearing so many jewels.

The *Voivode* wore a long crimson coat ornamented with gold buttons and yellow top-boots with gold spurs. On his head was a close-fitting lamb-skin hat.

In one hand he held a heavy axe, symbolic of his authority, in the other a whip with three leather thongs.

Jewelled daggers, stuck in the red sashes that all the gypsies wore round their waists, glistened in the firelight.

Red was the predominant colour of the many skirts, sometimes as many as seven, worn by the gypsy women, whose arms were encircled by dozens of jewelled bracelets, as were their ankles.

There was a large fire in the centre of a clearing and the gypsies were ranged round it in a circle, their tents hidden in the shadows under the trees.

Ilona and the Prince were led to a huge pile of coloured cushions on which they sat, where they were served a gypsy meal that was unlike anything Ilona had ever eaten before.

There were stews that had a succulent taste that she had never encountered even in French cooking.

There was special bread that the gypsies baked in their fires, and there was wine to drink in goblets made by the Kalderash, one of the gypsy tribes, set with amethysts, sapphires, carnelians, and quartz.

The *Voivode* made a speech to the Prince, thanking him for the protection that he had given the gypsies, and immediately when he had finished there was music.

It was music, as the Count had said, that was different from anything Ilona had heard before.

There was the trill of the *naiou,* or pipes of Pan, the twang of *cithara,* the beat of the tambourines.

But it was the violins that seemed to draw Ilona's heart from her body.

She knew that it was the union of two races, the Magyar and the Hungarian gypsies, that had produced this soul-stirring music.

Then the haunting melody swept away not only her unhappiness but also all the restrictions that she had felt all her life, in Paris and now in Dabrozka.

She felt as if the notes vibrated through her and set her whole being free. Then, as the dinner was finished and only the goblets of wine remained beside their places, the dancing began.

Now the music grew wilder, more passionate, more magnetic, more demanding, so that Ilona felt herself instinctively respond and her shoulders began to move with the rhythm of it.

Her eyes were shining in the light from the fire and they were very green. The flames picked out the red-gold of her hair and her lips were parted.

The dancers began slowly, the women first, while those who were not dancing sang a *kuruc* chant to the music, giving it rhythmic depth and a resonance that accentuated the beauty of the instruments.

The music grew wilder, and now as the dancers quickened their pace the men joined them.

Then from the crowd flashing round the fire, their jewels dazzling at the speed with which they moved, there came one dancer.

Ilona found it difficult to imagine that anyone could look so beautiful and at the same time so seductive with the feline grace of a panther.

She heard her name cried by the crowd: "Mautya" —"Mautya."

The gypsy had long dark hair hanging below her waist and her high cheek-bones and huge black eyes told Ilona that she was of Russian origin.

She began to dance the Zarabandas.

This was the famous snake-dance. Ilona had heard it spoken of with bated breath.

Her body swayed like the wind in the leaves, her skirts swirled round her bare legs, and her arms were an enticement, so that it was impossible not to watch the sensitive flexibility of her hands.

And her dark eyes, slanting a little at the corners,

flashed and seemed to be full of fire as her body moved first swiftly, leaping in the air, then slowly, sinuously, and seductively, so that there was the sensuousness of a serpent in every movement she made.

Then as the violins rose to a crescendo, as the dancer moved alone while the others leapt and twirled behind her, she held out both her hands invitingly towards the Prince.

There was no need for words.

Her flashing dark eyes and her red lips spoke for her.

It seemed to Ilona as if for a moment the music was silent, until as the Prince rose to his feet to take the outheld hands in his, there was a wild crescendo of sound that seemed to rise up into the starlit sky.

Then as Ilona watched him dancing as wildly as the gypsy herself, she knew despairingly that she loved him!

Chapter Five

Love came to Ilona not as a warm, exotic sense of joy, but as an all-consuming fire.

She felt it burn through her until, watching the Prince dancing with Mautya, she wanted to tear the woman from him, to strike her, to do her violent injury, even to murder her.

She had never in her whole sheltered life felt anything like the wildly conflicting emotions that transformed her whole body into a kind of battlefield!

She knew that her hands were trembling and her heart was beating tumultuously in her breast; but she felt too as if her eyes were flashing sparks of fire and her fingers were curved, ready to be at the gypsy's throat.

She loved the Prince! She loved him with an overwhelming, passionate jealousy that was unconfinable.

All the self-control that her mother had instilled into her since she was a small child vanished in a possessive desire to cry aloud that the Prince was hers!

He was her husband! He had married her and she felt prepared to fight every woman in the world to substantiate her claim.

"I love him! I love him!" she cried beneath her breath.

But it was a defiant declaration of war rather than the tender softness of a woman ready to surrender herself to a man.

For some minutes the Prince danced alone with the gypsy. Then as the music seemed to rise triumphant into the sky the others joined in.

The women's multitudinous skirts swirled round their bare legs, their anklets jingled as they leapt and gyrated over the soft ground, while their jewels, like their dark eyes, glittered in the light from the fire.

Only the older gypsies and the *Voivode,* who sat beside Ilona, did not join in the dancing.

Suddenly she felt the whole scene swinging dazzlingly in front of her eyes so that it became a waving kaleidoscope of colour and movement in which it was hard even to distinguish the Prince.

For one moment Ilona contemplated joining the dancers and forcing the Prince to be her partner.

Then despite the primitive emotions that possessed her, some remnant of pride made her bend towards the *Voivode* to say:

"I am rather tired. Will you excuse me if I return to the Castle?"

The gypsy Chief smiled as if he understood, and Ilona added quickly:

"I would not wish to interrupt His Highness's enjoyment. Perhaps I could leave without anybody being aware that I had gone."

The *Voivode* helped her to her feet and they moved into the shadows behind the silk-covered couch on which she had dined.

It was not far to the gate that led into the garden, and there waiting for her, as Ilona had expected, was one of the Prince's Aides-de-Camp and servants carrying torches.

She held out her hand to the *Voivode.*

"Thank you for a delightful and very exciting evening," she said. "Will you please convey my gratitude to your whole tribe?"

"You are very gracious," the gypsy said in his own language.

He raised the back of his hand to his forehead in an obeisance that proclaimed the gypsies' Eastern origin.

Without looking back at the dancers leaping against the red glow of the fire, Ilona walked towards the Castle accompanied by the Aide-de-Camp.

It seemed to her as she moved away that the music

was calling her, enticing her, and at the same time laughing mockingly.

She could still feel the fire it had evoked racing through her veins and making her breath come quickly between her lips.

She only hoped the Aide-de-Camp would think she was as quiet and composed as she had been during the four days she had lived at the Castle.

When she reached her bed-room Ilona flung open the window to stand looking out into the starlit darkness.

She could hear the music throbbing until it seemed to be part of the beat of her heart, exciting her and accentuating the love she had already acknowledged until it became utterly unbearable.

Sharply she closed the casement to shut out the haunting melody of the violins, but she could not erase the passions they had evoked within her heart and mind.

Long after Magda had left her and she was alone in the darkness, Iona lay tense, her whole body throbbing with a desperate, aching desire for the Prince.

She knew that he would not come to her room to-night, and she thought of him holding the gypsy Mautya in his arms and kissing those curved red lips that had smiled at him so invitingly.

She told herself that the Prince at twenty-eight would obviously have had many women in his life, and if the Russian gypsy was his mistress who would blame him?

Never had Ilona imagined that a woman could be so alluring, so seductive, with a magic mysticism about her that he would never find in any woman of his own class.

She tortured herself with remembering the hard possessiveness of his lips, and then imagining the gypsy returning his kiss as she had been unable to do.

Why had she not known then that he was the only man who would ever matter in her life?

Why, instead of hating him for touching her, had she not responded as she was sure any other woman would have done?

She thought of the quizzical, mocking look in his blue eyes and knew that, just as she now found him irresistible, there must have been many, many women who had felt the same.

"He hates and despises me," she told herself miserably, and went down to a special hell of unhappiness and despair at the thought.

It was impossible to sleep. All Ilona could think of was the gypsy in the Prince's arms and his mouth seeking hers.

"I love him! I love him!" she cried despairingly.

She might lack self-restraint. She might lack control, pride, and all the attributes of a lady that her mother had instilled into her so painstakingly.

But she knew that if the Prince had come to her room as he had done on other nights she would have flung herself down on her knees before him and implored him to kiss her.

"Mama would be ashamed of me!" Ilona told herself as dawn came.

Yet she could no more repress what she was feeling than she could prevent the sun rising over the mountains and shining golden on the waterfall behind the Castle.

She rang the bell for Magda long before her usual hour for being called, and when the maid had drawn back the curtains Ilona asked eagerly:

"What are the plans for today, Magda? Am I going driving with His Highness?"

She wanted to see him. She knew, however much it hurt her to think of where he had spent the night, that she wanted to be with him, to look at him even if he did not look at her, to hear his voice.

"At least I shall be beside him in the carriage," Ilona told herself. "At least I can watch him while he is charming and sympathetic to other people. At least with me he will not be with his gypsy mistress!"

But when Magda brought in Ilona's breakfast there was a note on it from Count Duzsa.

It was the regular method by which he informed Ilona of the day's programme.

Hastily she picked up the piece of paper and read:

His Highness has a meeting with the Prime Minister and the other members of the Council in Vitózi this morning. Perhaps Your Royal Highness would wish to go riding? His Highness will return at noon for luncheon.

Ilona's first feeling was one of disappointment that she would not see the Prince until luncheon-time. But at least, she thought irrepressibly, if he was with the Prime Minister he would not be with the gypsy.

"Please inform Count Duzsa," she said to Magda, "that I would like to ride in an hour's time."

She paused, then added:

"And tell him I wish to be accompanied only by a groom. I do not require a large escort."

She was thinking how, when she went riding from the Palace, there had been two Army officers and two grooms to take care of her.

She was sure the Prince would not expect her to endure so much formality when she was riding on Sáros land.

When she came downstairs, wearing a white pique riding-habit, which the Empress Eugénie had made fashionable before the last days of the Second Empire, Ilona looked extremely attractive.

She had thought when she glanced at herself in the mirror that it was a pity the Prince could not see her.

Then her heart dropped as she remembered that he was obviously not attracted by a woman who looked aristocratic but rather by one who wore the swirling skirts of a gypsy dancer, and had a barbaric, exotic beauty that she could never emulate.

Count Duzsa was waiting for her in the Hall.

"I have obeyed your wishes, Ma'am," he said. "You will be accompanied by only one groom, but may I respectfully suggest that you do not go too far?"

"Surely there is no danger for me riding in the woods on this side of the river?" Ilona enquired.

"No, of course not," Count Duzsa replied. "At the same time, I have a feeling that if we had asked His Highness he would have insisted on your being accompanied by one of the Aides-de-Camp."

"Today I wish to be alone," Ilona replied with a little smile.

"I understand," Count Duzsa said, "but please be very careful of yourself, Ma'am. You are very precious."

Ilona longed to retort: "Not to your master and my husband." But instead she thanked him quietly and set off from the Castle, followed by a middle-aged groom whom she had seen on other occasions.

He rode a few paces behind her and Ilona took a path running across the hill, which was sheltered by trees through which she had glimpses of the valley and the river below.

There were bridges over deep gorges and small cascades, and when the path divided, Ilona hesitated for a moment.

One way, she could see, led higher up the hillside towards the snow-capped mountains, while the other path plunged down into the valley and she could see a thick forest of pine-trees beneath her.

She suddenly thought she would like to revisit the place where she had first encountered the Prince. She had the idea that it was not far below where she now was.

She turned her horse's head and began the steep descent down the mountainside until she smelt the sweet fragrance of the pine-trees.

She remembered how she had come unexpectedly upon the men gathered together in the clearing and listened without understanding as they had protested to the Prince against her father's unjust and cruel laws.

It was easy to understand now that he had been obliged to meet them in secret so that the King would not learn that they were plotting against him.

And who could blame them, Ilona thought, for turning to the one man who would try to help them? The one man strong enough to defy her father's tyrannical, dictatorial rule?

She found the clearing and recognised it immediately.

There were the fallen logs on which many of the

men had been sitting, and the place at the far end from which the Prince had risen to come to her side.

She thought now that she must have known the moment she saw him that fate had brought him into her life, and it was inevitable that she should love him.

And yet at the time she had definitely resented the manner in which he had spoken to her, the authoritative way in which he had taken her horse's bridle and led her away from the clearing back towards the river.

And then . . .

Ilona shut her eyes.

She could almost feel the Prince lifting her from her horse, holding her tightly in his arms, and bending his head towards her.

"Why did I not know when he kissed me that I loved him and that I would never be able to escape from that love?"

Even as she asked herself the question a respectful voice beside her said:

"Excuse me, Your Royal Highness, but I think we should return to the Castle."

Ilona started. Lost in her thoughts, she had forgotten the groom was with her.

With an effort she came back to reality and asked:

"Is there any hurry?"

"I may be mistaken, Your Royal Highness, but I've a feeling that we're being watched!"

"Watched?" Ilona questioned. "By whom?"

The groom looked round nervously.

"It was soon after we left the Castle, Your Royal Highness. Of course I may be mistaken, but I think we would be wise to return."

"I cannot imagine who would be watching me," Ilona said, "but time must be getting on and I am quite prepared to go back."

She moved forward a few paces so that she could see the place where, after the Prince had kissed her, her horse had forded the river.

The level was a little lower than it had been a week ago. The water was silver and clear in the sunshine, and as she looked at it a salmon jumped and the ripples widened out towards the bank on the other side.

Then Ilona heard the groom give an exclamation.

On the opposite bank there were four horsemen riding down towards her and plunging into the water.

She stared at them in astonishment and as she did so she heard horses' hooves behind her and the sound of other horses coming through the trees.

She felt her heart give a sudden leap of fear.

She knew who the men approaching her were, knew them by their round lamb-skin hats and sleeveless sheep-skin coats.

They were the *Zyghes*, the savage horse-thieves who lived high up in the mountains.

They were the terror of every herdsman because they lived by stealing horses from the steppes, usually choosing those that were already half tamed, often injuring and sometimes killing the *Csikós* who were in charge of them.

The shepherds also hated them because the *Zyghes* lived off the land.

They stole the sheep they wished to eat, they drove away the cattle in the dark, and the fact that they lived in caves high in the mountains made it almost impossible to bring them to justice.

The *Zyghes* surrounded Ilona and she heard the groom give a cry as he was thrown off his horse.

Then before she could speak or do anything but stare at them with frightened eyes, one of the *Zyghes* had taken hold of her bridle and was pulling her horse across the river.

There was nothing Ilona could do but hold on to the pommel to prevent herself from falling off.

Another *Zyghe* came to her on the other side and as they reached the top of the bank they started to gallop wildly towards the open steppe.

Other *Zyghes* followed, bringing the groom's riderless horse, and Ilona knew that they must in fact have been following her ever since she left the Castle.

But why? For what reason?

She found it difficult to think as the horses galloped over the steppe, their hooves thundering on the green grass, the wind blowing in Ilona's face, making it difficult for her to be conscious of anything except the danger she was in.

They must have ridden for nearly a mile before a *Zyghe* behind them gave a yell, and the two men on either side of Ilona reined in their horses.

One of them looked back to shout:

"What is it?"

He spoke in a strange accent, but Ilona understood the words.

There was no need for the men following to explain.

The reins of the riderless horse had become entangled and were in danger of throwing the animal.

One man jumped down to release them and Ilona asked:

"W-what do you . . . want of me? Where are you . . . taking me?"

The *Zyghe* she addressed was a wild-looking man with long hair and a sweeping black moustache. His face had high Mongolian cheek-bones, which proclaimed his Magyar descent.

His dark eyes slanted a little at the corners and he looked at her in what she felt was an unpleasant manner as he replied:

"Money! You bring us plenty money!"

He slapped his hip as he spoke and Ilona stared at him in surprise.

"Do you mean . . . you are holding me for . . . ransom?"

She spoke clearly and slowly, hoping they would understand her pure Dabrozkan.

He shook his head.

"Money here!" he said, slapping his hip again, and now the others all roared with laughter.

For a moment Ilona could not understand what they were trying to say. Then suddenly she realised what must have happened.

Her father had paid these men—she was as sure of it as if they had actually said so!

It was his revenge on her for becoming a Sáros—an act of defiance that he intended to disconcert the Prince and undoubtedly cause consternation amongst the members of the Council.

It seemed incredible that he should do such a thing, but she knew that it was just the type of action that would please him, because no-one could have expected it.

He might possibly have made arrangements with the thieves to return her eventually to the Palace or even to her husband.

But in the meantime she would be forced to live with them in some dirty, primitive cave and to suffer the humiliation of knowing that she could not defy him as she had tried to do when he had beaten her into submission.

It was horrifying—it was diabolical! Nevertheless, Ilona thought despairingly, there was nothing whatever she could do about it.

The *Zyghes* were laughing and joking amongst themselves, and now one of them raised a hind leg of the groom's horse they had captured and discovered that in crossing the river he had picked up a stone.

The man drew a long, evil-looking knife from the sash that encircled his waist.

As the blade glinted in the sunshine Ilona averted her eyes, thinking how often it had killed a stolen animal or, worse still, wounded or murdered those who tried to protect their property.

She remembered all too well that the *Zyghes* were the bogey-men of the small villages of Dabrozka and their many crimes made them invariably spoken of with bated breath.

"How could Papa have done this to me?" she asked herself.

She wondered despairingly if anyone would know where she had gone, and if the groom had been too insensible to fetch help when they had thrown him from his horse.

Anyway, it would take him some time to walk back the way they had come, she thought, and if he tried to reach the city along the river-bank, the *Zyghes* would have taken her to their caves long before there was any chance of a rescue-party finding her.

Despite the sharp point of the *Zyghe's* knife, it was taking a long time to dislodge the stone that had embedded itself under the iron shoe, while the other five *Zyghes* sat watching.

They rode their horses without saddles and with bridles made of rope. Their animals were unshod and Ilona felt that they were perhaps inexperienced in dealing with shod animals.

"You say you have been given money to capture me," she said suddenly. "If you will take me back, I will see that you are given more money than you were first given. Much, much more!"

She thought they had difficulty in understanding what she was saying and she repeated herself several times.

"However much you have now," she said, "I give you two . . . no . . . three times as much if you take me back to the Castle."

In answer, one of the *Zyghes* put out a large dirty hand towards her, palm upwards.

She understood that he was asking for the money immediately, and she replied:

"I have no money with me, but there is much money waiting for you at the Castle."

She pointed to it far away in the distance and went on:

"You keep what you have, and I give you three times as much again!"

The *Zyghe* shook his head.

"Five times as much!" Ilona cried desperately.

Again he held out his hand, and she saw that there was dried blood on his fingers, as if he had recently killed an animal. It made her shudder.

"Money at the Castle," she said insistently.

The *Zyghe* turned his hand over slowly and the other men roared with laughter as if at some joke.

Ilona understood all too well what he was trying to say.

They would not risk going into danger. They did not believe they would be paid for taking her back and they might well lose the money they had already.

The man who had been attending to the horse's hoof gave a shout of triumph.

He had managed to extract the stone without prizing away the shoe itself, and now he sprang onto the back of his own horse and they all started to move forward.

Ilona looked back despairingly towards the Castle and as she did so she drew in her breath.

Far away in the distance she saw a black splodge against the green of the steppe and she felt sure it was a band of horsemen!

Hastily she turned her head so that she would not draw attention to what she had seen.

The *Zyghes* were laughing amongst themselves.

She realised they were sneering at her attempt to bribe them and telling one another it had only been a trap to bring them within range of the soldiers' rifles.

They were so intent on laughing and talking that, instead of galloping wildly as they had done when they first captured Ilona, they now moved comparatively slowly.

Their horses were trotting with the easy graceful movement that was characteristic of the Dabrozkan horses and which they could keep up for hours at a time without exhausting themselves.

The two men on either side of Ilona each had a hand on the bridle of her horse.

She held on to the pommel of her saddle, longing desperately to look back to see if she had been right in thinking that there were horsemen coming behind them, but knowing that to do so would alert her captors.

If ever she had found difficulty in controlling herself, it was now, when she was acutely aware that she might be rescued, and yet at the same time might have been mistaken in what she had seen.

They rode on, when suddenly one of the *Zyghes* behind gave a loud cry.

Ilona looked back and saw that she had not been mistaken.

Now, little more than a quarter of a mile away, a number of men were galloping towards them and she was sure that among them she had a glimpse of the uniform worn by the Prince's soldiers.

But she only had time for a mere glance before the

Zyghes had started to gallop wildly as they had done before.

Now they were whipping their horses and Ilona's to quicken their pace and she could only concentrate on staying in the saddle.

Her riding-hat was whisked from her head from the speed at which they were galloping and the wind, which blew directly in their faces, and there was nothing she could do to save it.

The *Zyghes* were bending low over their horses' necks, exhorting them with loud cries to further efforts and bringing down their whips persistently and cruelly on their horses' flanks.

Each time they hit Ilona's horse he jerked forward, and she felt that at any moment she might fall off and find herself trampled underfoot by those behind her.

Then incredibly she heard the sound of other horses drawing nearer and nearer to them.

Suddenly there was the sharp report of a pistol, and the man who was holding her bridle on the left toppled from his horse onto the ground.

Then another horse, still at full gallop, ranged beside hers and a strong arm lifted Ilona from the saddle and swept her through the air to land with a crash.

For a moment she was half unconscious at the impact.

Then with a sense of elation she realised that she was in the Prince's arms across the front of his saddle and her head was against his chest.

She knew as she gasped for breath that he had performed the feat that was most admired amongst Dabrozkan horsemen—that of lifting a person from one horse to another at full gallop!

Ilona gasped and found it hard to breathe; at the same time, her heart was singing because he was so strong and because he had saved her.

They galloped for quite a distance before the Prince brought his horse to a standstill, but Ilona, hiding her face against him, could only think that she was safe.

At least he had cared enough to rescue her.

* * *

Magda came from Ilona's bed-room to find the Prince waiting in the Sitting-Room.

She had heard someone knock very softly against the door and had risen from Ilona's bed-side to see who it was.

She closed the door behind her before she curtseyed and waited for the Prince to speak.

"How is she?" he asked in his deep voice.

"Her Royal Highness is sleeping."

"She is all right?"

"A little shaken. It must have been extremely frightening to be captured by the *Zyghes*."

"It must indeed," the Prince said. "But I am sure Her Royal Highness will soon recover, although it was such an unpleasant experience."

"*M'mselle* is not as strong as she looks, Your Highness," Magda said. "And is that strange, after suffering as she did in the Siege of Paris?"

The Prince was suddenly still.

"Are you telling me," he asked in a strange tone, "that Her Royal Highness was in the Siege of Paris?"

"I thought you knew, Your Highness," Magda replied. "That was where Her Majesty lived after we left Dabrozka."

"I had no idea," the Prince said as if he was speaking to himself. "I thought, although I must have been mistaken, that someone said you were living in Bordeaux."

Magda smiled.

"La Rue de Bordeaux, Your Highness! A little street near the Champs Élysées in Paris!"

"Her Royal Highness was in the Siege!" the Prince said as if he was trying to convince himself of the truth.

"It was terrible, Sire! It's a wonder we didn't starve to death. Do you know, Your Highness, that potatoes when one could get them were twenty-eight francs a bushel, and butter, which we never saw, was thirty-five francs a pound?"

The Prince smiled at the indignation in Magda's voice.

"I always heard that those who could afford it could

obtain food and I am sure you had plenty of money!"

"Plenty!" Magda's voice was almost a shriek. "We had only what Her Majesty owned personally, and that was little enough! We were in hiding, Your Highness—Madame Radák, and her daughter, little *M'mselle* Ilona. Who worried about us?"

"I had no idea," the Prince murmured.

"It was scrimp and save, scrimp and save, with Convent fees to pay! We scraped along," Magda went on. "Although *M'mselle* never would have had a new gown if I hadn't made her one from cheap material I bought in the market!"

The Prince did not speak and Magda continued:

"But we managed somehow until the Siege! Then it was often only a piece of dry bread and a drink of cold water. There was no fire to heat it!"

Magda paused, and there was an almost agonising note in her voice as she said:

"It was the cold that winter which killed Her Majesty. I would hear her coughing night after night! Even after the Siege was over, she went on coughing her life away but she never complained."

Magda looked up at the Prince and her eyes pleaded with him.

"Be careful of *M'mselle,* Your Highness! Like her mother, she'll never complain. She's been taught to be proud—never to admit to suffering, whatever it might be."

Magda drew in her breath.

"Not even when His Majesty beat her, as he had beaten her mother often enough, did she tell me the truth. 'I had a fall, Magda,' she says, as if I wouldn't know a whip-lash when I saw one."

"His Majesty beat her?"

The Prince's question rang out like a pistol-shot.

"You must have seen her back, Your Highness," Magda replied. "It's a mass of bruises! How she managed to smile on her wedding-day, I'll never know!"

The Prince did not speak, and after a moment Magda said nervously:

"You will not tell Her Royal Highness that I've spoken to you of this? She would be very angry. All the years in the Palace when I would have to undress Her Majesty and put her to bed after she had been beaten unconscious, she would never speak of what had happened."

"The King is mad!" the Prince exclaimed violently.

"Yes, Your Highness, but it is not entirely his fault."

The Prince looked at Magda in surprise and she explained:

"Few people are aware of it, but when His Majesty was a child he was dropped by his nurse. The servants were too frightened, as the nurse was, to speak of the accident to His Majesty's parents."

"It must have injured his brain," the Prince said almost beneath his breath.

"That's what I always thought, Your Highness, and that's why, when His Majesty becomes angry, he's not human. He's as savage and as dangerous as a wild animal."

Magda's lips tightened as she said:

"If only you knew some of the things I've seen, some of the things that happened at the Palace! But at least my little *M'mselle* has escaped!"

"Yes," the Prince said quietly. "She has escaped!"

* * *

Ilona awoke late in the afternoon and when she stirred Magda rose to pull back the curtains and let in the afternoon sunshine.

"I must have . . . slept for a . . . long time," Ilona murmured.

"Do you feel better, dearie?"

"I am perfectly well," Ilona replied. "But I did not sleep last night, and that is why I was so tired."

"Yes, of course," Magda agreed, "and now I will fetch you something to eat. The Chef has been making you some nourishing soup and is ready to cook anything else you fancy."

"Do not bring me too much," Ilona said. "It will soon be dinner-time and you know what delicious food we have here in the evening."

Magda was not listening. She had hurried to the door.

When Ilona was alone she sat up and stretched, feeling as if she embraced the whole room because she was safe and because the Prince had ridden back with her in his arms.

She had been fully conscious but she wanted to stay as she was, and so had made no effort to say she was unharmed and well enough to ride.

He had given her a feeling of safety and protection that she had never known before. It had been a wonderful thrill to rest her head against his shoulder and feel his arm holding her closely against him.

It was worth every moment of her terror when captured by the *Zyghes* to know that the Prince had defeated their intention of keeping her prisoner, whoever had instigated it.

One of the *Zyghes* had been killed and another badly injured in the skirmish with the Prince's rescue-force.

The rest had been taken prisoner.

Ilona, since she was no longer in their power, would not have cared if they had gone free. She kept her eyes shut and wished the ride back to the Castle had taken far longer than it did.

When someone had lifted her down from the front of the Prince's saddle, she could have cried out in misery at leaving him. Then as she realised that Count Duzsa was holding her she heard the Prince say:

"I will carry Her Royal Highness upstairs."

She had felt a rapturous thrill of excitement run through her as once again she was in his arms.

He held her very close. As he climbed the staircase she could hear his spurs jingling, making a music that seemed to accompany the singing of her heart.

He had not entrusted her to a servant or even to the Count!

He was himself carrying her up to her room, and she wished that she was brave enough to tell him that she wanted him to stay with her, that she wanted to talk to him.

But Magda, the Housekeeper, and a number of other

maids were waiting at the top of the staircase and when the Prince had laid her down on her bed he walked away and left her to their ministrations.

"He saved me!" Ilona cried to herself now. "He saved me! As long as I can be with him I can bear his coldness and even his indifference."

Then the thought of Mautya, the gypsy, was like the stab of a dagger in her breast.

'Perhaps tonight he will stay with her again!' Ilona thought miserably.

It was some time before Magda returned and even as she set the tray with its numerous silver dishes down beside the bed, Ilona knew there was something wrong.

She had been so close to Magda for so many years that she could sense without words everything she was feeling, could read every inflection of her voice and every expression in her eyes.

"What is wrong, Magda?" she asked.

"Drink your soup, M'mselle."

Ilona took a sip, found it delicious, and took another.

"Something has upset you," she said.

"Is it surprising?" Magda asked evasively.

Ilona drank a little more soup.

"It must be something that has happened since you left the room. When I talked to you just now you were so glad that I was alive and safe!"

"I am still glad about that," Magda answered. "Eat, my child. You need to renew your strength."

Ilona finished the soup and ate a few mouthfuls of a pink-fleshed salmon that she knew would have been caught in the river that morning.

Then she drank a little of the golden wine that Magda had poured into a glass before she said:

"Now tell me, Magda. What has happened?"

There was silence and she said firmly:

"I insist upon knowing!"

She had a terrifying feeling that it was something that concerned the Prince.

Had he left the Castle? Had Magda found out something unpleasant about him and the gypsy?

She waited apprehensively and after a moment Magda said reluctantly:

"It's the Russians, *M'mselle!*"

"The Russians?" Ilona repeated in astonishment.

"The servants are saying that the Prince learnt that His Majesty has invited them into the country to occupy the Palace!"

"It cannot be . . . true!"

"His Highness has said nothing, *M'mselle*, but the officers have been talking amongst themselves and the Major-Domo overheard them say that if the Russians can get their guns into the Palace they can bombard Vitózi and us!"

Ilona was very still.

She could remember the horrors of the bombardment of Paris, the noise and the devastation caused by the German shells, the people who had been killed and wounded, and the terror that every outburst of firing evoked.

"It is impossible!" she said aloud.

But she knew even as she spoke that what Magda had told her was only too possible.

If Russian guns were installed in the Palace, standing so high above the valley, nowhere within their range of fire would be safe.

"What is . . . being done?" she asked.

"Members of the Council and the officers of His Highness's Army are discussing the position at this moment," Magda replied. "But you, my little *M'mselle*, must be taken away to safety. I will tell His Highness that myself!"

Ilona jumped out of bed.

"I will speak to His Highness. Quick, Magda, give me my velvet négligée."

Magda looked at her in astonishment.

"But, *M'mselle*, His Highness is in conference."

"I have no time too dress," Ilona said impatiently. "Just do as I say, Magda!"

She spoke in a peremptory way, which was very unlike her, and Magda ran to the wardrobe and brought from it one of the exquisite négligées they had bought in Paris.

This one was intended for the colder weather and was of turquoise-blue velvet, trimmed with row upon row of white lace inset with turquoise ribbons.

Ilona had not worn it before, and she put it on hastily.

She buttoned it down the front, slipped her feet into her slippers, which were lying beside a chair, and without even glancing in the mirror she ran towards the door.

"Where are you going, *M'mselle?* You cannot go downstairs dressed like that!" Magda cried.

But Ilona did not listen to her.

Running along the corridor, she hurried down the staircase and found the Major-Domo in the Hall.

He looked at her in astonishment and she said:

"Where is His Highness?"

"He is in the Hunting-Room, Your Royal Highness. Shall I inform him that you wish to see him?"

Ilona did not answer. She did not even hear the end of the sentence. She was running straight to the Hunting-Room.

It was a fine Reception-Room on the ground floor, large enough for dances or entertainments, and also used for conferences and meetings.

Two footmen were standing outside the double doors and they were so surprised at Ilona's appearance that it was only when she had actually reached them that they remembered to open the doors for her.

She walked into the room.

There were thirty or forty men present, seated in chairs, facing the Prince. He was sitting at a table with a senior Army officer on one side of him, and on the other an elderly man whom Ilona thought she had seen with the Prime Minister.

They were talking earnestly, but at Ilona's entrance there was a sudden silence.

She did not even look at the men who stared at her in surprise as they rose to their feet. Her eyes were on the Prince's face as he too rose.

For a moment his self-possession seemed to desert him as he saw the way Ilona was dressed—her red hair streaming loose over her shoulders, her green eyes seeking his.

She reached the table in front of him and stood looking up into his eyes to ask:

"Is it true that the Russians have entered the country and have occupied the Palace?"

"That is what I have been told," the Prince said quietly. "But there is no need for you to be frightened."

"I am not frightened," Ilona said scornfully. "I have come to tell you how you can enter the Palace and take them by surprise before they can fire on us!"

She saw the astonishment in the Prince's face. Then the Army officer beside him asked:

"Is there a way into the Palace, Your Royal Highness, without approaching it from the valley?"

Ilona knew he was thinking of how the Palace had repelled many enemy assaults in the past, thanks to its strong fortifications and lofty position from which the defenders could fire down with a devastating loss of life on anyone approaching the gates.

"There is a way into the Palace," Ilona replied, "which only I know. I doubt if even my father is aware that it exists."

Ever since Magda had told her that the Russians were being admitted into the Palace she had been thinking about the secret that Julius had imparted to her so many years ago.

He had been sixteen at the time, and the King had discovered that he had been out at night enjoying himself in the Inns in Vitózi where there was dancing and drinking and many pretty girls to entertain the customers.

There had been a row that reverberated through the Palace when her father, as usual, indulged himself in one of his tyrannical rages.

The King had threatened to beat Julius, who had immediately picked up a sword and offered to fight his father.

That he should be defied by his own son had infuriated the King to the point where he might even have killed Julius had it not been for the Queen's intervention.

Finally Julius had been punished by being locked in his room by his Tutor and told that if he went out again at night without his father's permission he would be placed in one of the dungeons and chained to the wall.

Ilona, then age nine, had found her mother in tears and had gathered from what the Courtiers said and the chatter of the servants exactly what had happened.

What had upset her was that Julius had not only been locked in his room, but her father had also given instructions that he was to be given nothing to eat for the next twenty-four hours!

When she had been put to bed at her usual hour she found she could not sleep.

She waited until her Nurse had left the Nursery, doubtless to gossip with the other members of the staff. Then putting her pillows under the bed-clothes to make it look as if she were still there, she put on her dressing-gown and tip-toed along the passage to Julius's room.

It was very quiet and there appeared to be no-one about as she knocked tentatively at the door.

"Who is it?" Julius asked.

"It is me—Ilona!"

He had come to the door so that he could talk to her through the key-hole.

"I am locked in, Ilona."

"I know. Are you very hungry, Julius?"

"Very hungry, and very cross," he answered. "Where is the key of the door?"

Ilona looked round her and saw it hanging on a nail above her head.

She told Julius where it was.

"Can you reach it?"

"If I put a chair underneath it I can."

"Then let me out," Julius pleaded. "I will not let you get into trouble—I promise!"

"I am not afraid," she answered.

She pulled a chair into position, climbed onto it, lifted down the key, and opened the door.

Julius came out, picked her up in his arms, and kissed her.

He was tall for his age and looked very much older than his sixteen years.

The men of Dabrozka developed young and Julius was already a man.

"Thank you, Ilona," he said.

"Where are you going?" she asked.

"Out!" he replied. "You do not suppose I am going to let Papa keep me shut up like a rat in a trap?"

"He will be very angry if he catches you!"

"I know," Julius replied, "and that is why I am going to ask you to help me, Ilona."

"You know I will help you . . . you know I will!" Ilona replied eagerly.

Julius hung the key back on the nail and replaced the chair that Ilona had moved.

"If I come and wake you up," he asked, "will you lock me in again?"

"You know I will," Ilona answered. "But how are you going to get out of the Palace? The sentries will see you."

"Not the way I intend to go," he replied.

Ilona had realised it was a secret, and because she pleaded with him, Julius had good-humouredly taken her with him down a twisting staircase that was seldom used and led to the cellars.

This very old part of the Palace with its thick walls and uneven floors was not in use.

But Julius had found an old passageway that must have been built hundreds of years ago and which burrowed under the ground to emerge hidden by some rocks at the back of the Palace where people seldom went.

He had not shown Ilona the whole passage the first night, but after she had let him out subsequently half a dozen other times, she had managed to persuade him to take her down the passage in the day-time.

He had shown her how well the entrance was concealed between some boulders and beneath the thick branches of the acacia-trees.

"It is a secret between us," Julius had said. "You will never speak of it to anyone or I am certain Papa will cut off my head!"

"You know I would never betray you," Ilona had said adoringly.

And she had never mentioned the secret passage, not even to her mother.

She explained now to the Prince where it was and how it was possible to enter the passage from the outside without anyone in the Palace being aware of it.

"It is not overlooked and there are no rooms in use in that part of the building," she said.

Her eyes were fixed on the Prince and she spoke as if addressing him alone.

There was a silence in the room and everyone else was listening.

When she had finished the Prince took her hand in his and raised it to his lips.

"Thank you," he said quietly.

"This changes everything, Your Highness," the Army officer said excitedly.

"I must . . . come with you," Ilona said to the Prince.

He shook his head.

"That is impossible!"

"Then you will never find the entrance."

He hesitated and she went on:

"You know as well as I do you cannot afford to waste time, nor can you risk being seen by daylight."

"It is true that we shall have to enter the Palace as soon as it is dark," the Prince agreed.

"Then I will show you the way," Ilona insisted.

She saw his lips tighten as if once again he was going to refuse to take her into danger. Then she said, addressing the officer at his side:

"I am sure, Colonel, you will agree that we should move as soon as it is dark enough to conceal our movements. That will be in about an hour's time. I will go and get ready!"

She turned to walk from the room.

As she did so the men who had been listening to her spontaneously cheered her.

As the door closed behind her, a babble of excited voices burst out.

Chapter Six

Ilona ran back to the bed-room to find Magda waiting for her with a shocked expression on her face.

"Really, *M'mselle!*" she said in the tone of a scolding Nanny. "How could you go downstairs wearing little more than a négligée! What will His Highness think of you with your hair all over your shoulders?"

Ilona nearly retorted that His Highness was not interested in her or her hair one way or the other, and that his preference was for long dark locks that fell below the waist.

Instead, she said:

"Magda, I have to be dressed and ready as quickly as possible. I require a riding-habit!"

"You are going riding at this hour?" Magda exclaimed. "It is too much on top of what you have already gone through today!"

"I am all right! I am perfectly all right!" Ilona replied.

Refusing to listen to Magda's protests and grumbles, she began to dress herself as swiftly as she could.

She would have put on the first thing that came to hand, but Magda sensibly chose a riding-habit of deep sapphire velvet, and as Ilona covered her crisp white petticoats with the skirt she realised that it was a wise choice.

It was important that she should not be conspicuous, as she would be if she wore a lighter colour.

What was more, it would be cold once the sun had set and the winds carried the chill of the snows from the mountains.

As Magda arranged her hair, drawing it back neatly and tightly into the chignon she always wore when riding, Ilona looked at her high-crowned, fashionable hat and said:

"I have an idea, Magda! Did you pack that cloak I used to wear when we lived in Paris?"

"That old thing?" Magda replied scornfully. "I meant to throw it away or give it to some poor beggar, but the beggars here are better-dressed than we were in the past!"

"I will wear it!" Ilona said.

Magda tried to dissuade her but Ilona knew that the black woollen cloak with its hood would be just what she required as an effective disguise, and there would also be no need to wear a riding-hat.

All the time she was dressing her brain was busy planning how to approach the Palace without being seen, which meant, she knew, a long detour.

She was quite certain that if the Russians were already in the Palace, they would have sentries watching for the approach of troops from Vitózi.

As soon as the moonlight illumined the valley, anyone moving on the twisting road that wound from the river to the Palace gates would be easily discernible.

She was certain that the Prince and the Army officers themselves would have thought of this. At the same time, she felt responsible for the whole campaign.

"How could Papa do anything so unpatriotic, so wicked, as to intrigue with the Russians against his own people?" Ilona asked herself.

But she was well aware that the King when he was in one of his fanatical and tyrannical rages would do anything, however reprehensible, to get his own way.

It was all part of his vendetta against the Sáros and particularly Prince Aladár.

He could not forget or forgive the fact that he had been forced to allow his daughter to be married to his most despised enemy.

Nothing else would seem to him to be of any consequence.

Therefore, if the Russians had approached him, as Ilona was sure they had after learning that their plans for creating a civil war in Dabrozka had been thwarted, then the King would have acquiesced in anything they suggested.

Even though Ilona understood her father's anger, his behaviour was still incredible. Nevertheless, she did not doubt for a moment that the reports of what was happening were true.

What was really of importance now was time.

The pass over the mountains from Russia into Dabrozka was treacherous and narrow.

It would be impossible for a large number of men to enter the country quickly and without being detected.

What had happened, Ilona was sure, was that small groups of soldiers doubtless on horseback had infiltrated under cover of night.

They would have made their way over the narrow, rough road to the Palace to be welcomed by her father.

Once the Palace was in their hands and they had established their guns, it would be easy for the Russians to command all the known approaches and ensure a safe passage for the rest of their troops.

'We can prevent this from happening, if Aladár's men can take the Palace,' Ilona thought.

When finally she was dressed she left behind a tearful and protesting Magda and hurried downstairs to find everything in a buzz of activity.

Senior officers were consulting maps and giving orders to their juniors, horses were saddled and waiting in the court-yard, and Ilona could see through the open door that there were a number of mules with small, portable guns strapped to their backs.

She stood looking round her, the red of her hair heightened by the blue of her riding-habit.

She carried her black cloak over her arm.

Count Duzsa crossed the Hall to her side.

"I have been told of the secret passage, Ma'am," he said. "Can you remember, when you last saw it, whether it was well-built enough to have remained passable after all these years?"

Ilona smiled.

"It had not collapsed, Count, during the hundreds of years since it was built, and I therefore cannot believe that the last nine would have made much difference!"

"No, you are right, Ma'am," the Count conceded. "Maybe I am over-anxious, but I am trying to decide what implements our forces would need if they had to clear away stones and rubble."

"I am quite confident we shall find that the passage my brother showed me is easily negotiable," Ilona replied.

She thought for a moment, then said:

"It seemed very large to me at the time, but certainly Julius could stand upright in it and he was tall, nearly as tall at sixteen as the Prince is now!"

"And the width?" the Count asked.

"I should imagine it would be possible for at least two men to move abreast in it at the same time."

"Thank you, Ma'am," Count Duzsa said.

He moved from her side to convey the information she had given him to an Army officer and Ilona could see the relief on his face.

There was no sign of the Prince, but after Ilona had been in the Hall for about five minutes he came in through the front door, giving instructions as he did so to an officer who walked at his side.

He saw Ilona and came towards her. She felt her heart start to beat frantically.

"You are sure you are well enough to accompany us?" he asked.

"I will not allow you to go without me!" Ilona replied.

"It will be cold."

"I have a warm cloak."

"I see you have thought of everything!"

There was a note in his voice that was different from the way in which he had spoken to her before, but as she looked up at him questioningly there was an officer at his side and he turned away to give an order.

The sun had sunk and dusk was falling when finally they left the Castle.

Ilona had learnt, not from the Prince but from one of the officers, that the main body of the Sáros Army had already left.

They had moved off nearly an hour ago to intercept any other Russian troops who might be entering the country through the pass.

They had a long march ahead of them, as they too must approach their objective by a tortuous route.

Those who were left behind were thirty of the Prince's most trusted body-guard. These he intended to lead into the Palace once Ilona had shown them the secret passage.

When she heard what had been planned, she could not help a sudden tremor of fear for the Prince's life.

She did not expect him to be anywhere but in the forefront of the battle, because she knew that he would not ask any man to take greater risks than he himself was prepared to undertake.

But she felt desperately afraid lest he should die in his attempt to save Dabrozka.

Everything that happened tonight was crucial.

On it hinged the whole independence and sovereignty of their country.

There was no doubt that once the Russians got control it would be impossible to dislodge them. Neither Austria nor Hungary, nor Romania, would contemplate an all-out war against the whole might of the Tsar's Army.

Yet even so, with the country united, they might have been able to fight the Russians as the Caucasians had fought under Shammel for years before they were finally defeated.

But the people of Dabrozka were not united and their King had betrayed them.

It was bitterly humiliating for Ilona to realise that it was her father, a Radák, who had turned traitor in such a despicable and unspeakable manner.

His action would justify every complaint the Sáros had made against him, and she was well aware that they were as bitter and as vengeful in their dislike of the Radáks as her father was of them.

Yet the Prince had never mentioned or refuted the accusations that the King had brought against him of being implicated in the murder of Julius.

Ilona had expected that he would deny that, if nothing else.

But silence had been part of his defence, that cold, impenetrable, icy silence in which he remained frozen whenever they were alone.

She had learnt the truth from the Count.

She had not spoken of it until the third day after her arrival at the Castle. He had come to her Sitting-Room to discuss the guests who would be at dinner that evening.

"Will you tell me something, Count?" she asked.

"If it is within my power to do so, Ma'am."

"I want to know how my brother died."

The Count was silent and Ilona said:

"Please tell me. My father has accused the Sáros of killing him deliberately and with intent, which I am sure is untrue."

"It is a lie, Ma'am!"

"I was sure of it! But at the same time, I would wish to know what actually happened."

"It might distress you."

"It could not be worse than wondering, conjecturing, and inventing explanations of his death," Ilona replied.

The Count nodded.

"I am sure that is true. What we imagine is often so much worse than the reality."

"Then tell me about Julius," Ilona pleaded.

"There was a band of young men led, we learnt later, by Prince Julius, who found it amusing to go to the local Inns patronised by the Sáros and cause trouble."

Ilona drew in her breath.

She could imagine her brother, head-strong, daring, and bored with the gloom and restrictions of the Palace, finding such an escapade amusing.

"Sometimes they were quite light-hearted," the Count went on, "and although a certain amount of damage was done in the Inns by glasses and bottles being broken, the landlords were amply compensated and therefore not disposed to complain."

Ilona's eyes were on his face as the Count continued:

"As you can imagine, it was inevitable that some of the Sáros young men should consider it their duty to form a rival group to challenge the Radáks and fight them wherever they appeared."

The Count paused before he said reflectively:

"At first, I am sure, it was just a game: the rival groups had to be intelligent enough to guess where their enemies would appear and try to be in positions of advantage before they arrived."

His voice was grave as he went on:

"Then things began to get out of hand. I have no way of estimating what the casualties were amongst the Radáks, but a number of Sáros youths lost their lives or were badly injured."

"They used knives?" Ilona asked.

"And pistols!" the Count replied. "In fact the encounters became shooting-matches in which innocent by-standers, who had only gone to the Inn for a glass of wine after a hard day's work, were killed or wounded."

Ilona clasped her hands together.

She could understand all too well how easily such an explosive situation would escalate into what must have amounted to open war-fare.

"Your brother was killed in a small Inn near the river where there had never been any trouble before. The landlord catered mostly for courting couples who sat in arbours in his garden, drinking the local wine and making love."

He paused before he said sadly:

"Three betrothed men, all decent, industrious workers, were killed the same night as your brother died and six of the Sáros group."

"And the Radáks?" Ilona enquired.

"Besides your brother, four men were killed, one blinded, and another lost his leg!"

Ilona gave a little cry of horror.

"Your brother's identity was not known until the following morning after the bodies had been taken to the local Church for their relatives to claim them."

It had been a senseless way for Julius to throw away his life, Ilona thought.

Yet she could understand that he found such nightly excursions exciting and entertaining simply because he must have been so bored at the Palace.

She did not suppose that as he grew older he had found it any easier to put up with his father's autocratic behaviour, and she suspected that the King might have become jealous of his son.

There were many explanations and many excuses that could be made for Julius's death.

But the fact remained that he had thrown away his life in a manner that had helped no-one and had merely made the gulf between the Sáros and the Radáks even wider than it had been before.

"Thank you for telling me," Ilona said quietly to the Count, and they had gone on to speak of other things.

Riding away from the Castle through the darkness, Ilona thought now that perhaps because Julius had shown her the secret passage he would in fact be instrumental in saving Dabrozka.

"How did you ever learn of this?" she had asked.

Her brother had taken her through the passage and shown her the concealed entrance, which was indiscernible unless one was actually looking for it.

"You remember old Giskra?" he had asked.

"Yes, of course," Ilona answered.

Giskra had been Julius's first valet once he had become too old to be looked after by a Nanny.

He had served their grandfather and had always seemed to Ilona to be incredibly ancient.

He looked in fact like a little gnome, and as a child she had thought there were numbers of Giskras working away in the mountains, chiselling out the amethysts and other precious stones that her mother had treasured.

Giskra had adored Julius and had followed him about like a faithful spaniel, asking nothing more of life than the opportunity to serve him.

"Giskra learnt of the passage through grandfather," Julius told Ilona. "He had apparently wished to examine it one day and Giskra had gone with him to hold the lantern."

"And Giskra told you?"

"He took me down it when I wanted to go fishing and Papa had forbidden me to leave the Palace."

"For any good reason?" Ilona enquired.

Julius shrugged his shoulders.

"You know Papa. Any reason that is disagreeable and unjust is good in his eyes!"

The Prince had crossed the river a long way from the Palace and now as they left Sáros land Ilona felt frightened.

Supposing the King's Armies had anticipated that the Prince would oppose the Russians in defiance of orders to the contrary?

They might be hidden, ready to ambush the Sáros troops, and, if the Dabrozkans fought each other, that would be exactly what the Russians wanted.

But the woods near the river were very quiet. The trees were not so thick and there were no dense pine-forests as on the other side. But at least they sheltered the troops from observation.

The only noise was the jingle of the bridles and the breathing of the horses blowing through their nostrils.

Before they left the Prince had said:

"We move in silence. As you all know, voices carry, especially at night. No-one will speak unless it is absolutely necessary, and then only to an officer."

The Prince's band of thirty men were all mounted.

They wore dark Cavalry cloaks over their uniforms and beneath them every man had a pistol at his belt and there was a rifle strapped to his horse's saddle.

So that they would move more quietly the Prince had ordered them all to remove their spurs.

Dabrozkans were such magnificent riders that spurs were nothing more than a decorative part of their uniform.

No Dabrozkan riding for pleasure or dressed as a civilian ever wore spurs.

Despite the fact that they had crossed the river, there was still a long way to go.

They had to make a great detour over land that was first wooded, then rough and uneven, covered with huge boulders from some volcanic past.

It would have been impossible to travel quickly, even in the day-time.

At night it meant that every step might mean a twisted fetlock or a fall, even for the sure-footed Dabrozkan horses, which were used to such terrain.

They must have been travelling for an hour and a half before the Prince rode to Ilona's side.

She was vividly aware of him as he drew his horse alongside hers.

Now the moon was rising in the sky, and although its light was still pale and not of the strength it would be later she could see his face and the outline of his handsome features.

His eyes were pools of darkness and she could not guess at the expression in them.

He put out his hand to lay it on her arm and she felt herself quiver as if her whole body came alive at his touch.

"You are all right?"

He spoke almost beneath his breath, and rather than break the silence, she nodded, then smiled at him because she was so happy.

He had remembered her and he was concerned with her well-being.

Then she told herself that perhaps it was only because she had her uses and if she should collapse now they would be unable to find the passage into the Palace.

He removed his hand, but Ilona had an irrational impulse to hold on to him, to ask him to carry her on the front of his saddle as he had done earlier in the day.

Even to think of the sense of protection and safety he had given her was to feel a thrill of fire run through her.

His arm had been very strong and she had been

able to put her head on his shoulder and feel the roughness of his tunic against her cheek.

"I love him!" she told herself. "I love him so . . . overwhelmingly that even if we are both . . . killed tonight it will not matter as long as I am . . . with him!"

She thought that even the guns would no longer make her afraid as the German shells had done when they bombarded Paris.

Then, because her mother did not expect her to show any emotion, she had sat in the Sitting-Room of the small house, sewing.

She had forced herself not to start or wince when they heard the loud report and the crash of the exploding shell.

She had gone with Magda sometimes to see the devastation that the bombardment had caused—the shattered skeletons of great buildings with their mangled and torn fragments of iron looked desolate and at the same time menacing.

Yet she had known that the German shells, filled only with black powder, which could be heard all too plainly in the centre of Paris, had a demoralising effect that was a more potent weapon of war than was the damage they caused.

The Parisians had screamed hysterically and run for cover, the women herding their children frantically below ground into cellars and basements.

Only her mother remained completely rigid and expressionless when a shell fell within a hundred yards of their house, and Ilona after one frightened gasp had gone on with her embroidery.

She thought of the nights when she had listened, tense and apprehensive, and the days when to count the time between one shell and another had seemed interminable.

There was the same hollow feeling of fear within her now and yet it was a comfort she could not express to know that the Prince was near her.

'He is so magnificent, so fine and noble,' she thought. 'No wonder his men adore him!'

He rode to the front of his troops, leading the way

and finding every possible cover for them, whether consisting of trees or boulders.

Then at length when they had been riding for well over three hours Ilona saw the Palace to the left of them.

They had moved in a half-circle since they had left the Castle, and, having crossed the road to the pass, which had been a dangerous moment, they were moving in less difficult country and gradually approaching the Palace from the back.

The trees were very thick round its base and it was an awe-inspiring and frightening sight as the moonlight revealed it, looking almost like a fortified town above the tops of the trees.

Ilona knew how strongly the walls had been built and that the Palace was capable of withstanding a long siege, if necessary.

She began to wonder frantically how many Russians were already inside.

She could only pray that the Prince had received his information before too many of their enemies had installed themselves and their guns.

No-one had said so, but Ilona was certain that it was the gypsies who had carried the vital information to the Castle.

Her father's harshness and the manner in which he had exiled them would have turned them bitterly against him.

They would have been only too glad to inform the Prince of anything that might discredit the King.

Gypsies could move surreptitiously and with a secrecy that ensured their going undetected by even the most watchful soldiers.

They had been persecuted for so many years and in so many countries and they had learned how to escape into the woods and mountains where no-one was able to follow them.

'The gypsies would have told Aladár about the Russians,' Ilona thought, and wondered if their spokesman had been the alluring, exotic Mautya.

He would have been overwhelmingly grateful to her

and to her people. How would he have shown his gratitude?

The answer to the question was so painful that Ilona wanted to cry out in her distress.

Then she told herself severely that this was no moment for jealousy, no moment to be consumed, as she had been the night before, by a murderous hatred for the woman she suspected of being her husband's mistress.

"All that matters is that we should succeed and that Aladár should remain unhurt," she told herself.

They were now less than four hundred yards from the Palace and the Prince brought his horse to a halt.

Quietly the whole troop dismounted and gathered round the Prince, leaving six men to stay with the animals, who were furnished with nose-bags to keep them quiet.

An officer helped Ilona to the ground and she walked to the Prince's side.

She waited for his instructions.

"You will show me the entrance to the passage," he said in a low voice. "Then when we have entered you will return with Captain Gayozy to the Castle."

"I have no wish to do that," Ilona replied.

"Captain Gayozy has my orders," the Prince answered, "and you will please obey them. I will not risk your being in any danger."

Ilona said nothing.

She wanted to go on arguing with the Prince, but she realised that although they were speaking in very low voices it was possible for the officers near them to overhear what they were saying.

"Shall we go now?" she asked.

"We will go together," the Prince answered.

He took her hand as he spoke, as if she were a child being taken for a walk, and they moved ahead of the troops.

Ilona felt herself tremble as he touched her.

She had taken off one of her riding-gloves to push back her hood from her face and she had not replaced it.

Her fingers were cold while the Prince's were warm

and she thought that if only he loved her this would be an exciting adventure to tell their children.

Then she thought despairingly that they would have no children, and when the drama of the night was over, provided that they were both alive, the Prince had his mistress waiting for him, while she had nothing and no-one.

Owing to the trees, the back of the Palace was in deep shadow, and for one frantic moment, as they drew near to it, Ilona thought she had forgotten where the entrance was.

She had only been nine when she was last here and it was nine years since Julius had told her the secret of it.

Then it had been an exciting game, but naturally she had not thought about it again since she left Dabrozka.

As if with a perception she had not suspected, the Prince seemed to know what she was feeling, and his fingers tightened on hers.

"There is no hurry," he whispered almost beneath his breath. "Take your time. It may have become overgrown."

His voice dispersed the feeling of fear and swept away Ilona's uncertainty.

Now she was sure that the entrance was a little to the left, obscured by rocks and hidden beneath the flowering creeper that crawled over the base of the Palace like a green veil.

The Prince let her lead him and then when she pointed he pulled the creeper aside, revealing what appeared to be an iron grille.

It was easily moved and behind it was the entrance to the passage, just as Ilona remembered it.

There was no door, merely a narrow opening through which only one man could squeeze at a time, but which immediately opened into an enormous cave. The passage began at the back of it.

Ilona remembered that it went straight, rising slightly for some distance, then there were stone steps rising to another level and yet another, until a door opened into the part of the Palace that was never used.

It was where the dungeons were and huge cellars, which had once housed wine but which had been abandoned for more accessible storage-places near the Dining-Hall.

The Prince and Ilona had entered the cave and they were joined, one by one, by the soldiers.

Then the guns were passed through the opening and candle-lanterns gave a fitful glow carefully shaded so that they could not be seen from the out-side.

At last everyone was in the cave and the Prince turned to Ilona.

"Ride home as quickly as you can," he said quietly.

She did not reply and she thought that he looked down at her in the semi-darkness as if he waited for her to speak.

Then drawing his pistol from his belt he moved through the waiting men to lead them up the passage that loomed dark ahead of them.

Ilona watched them go, the last to leave being the men with the guns, which the mules had carried on their backs.

The officers following the Prince had taken the lan-terns with them, and now there was only the light from the narrow opening, which seemed, after the darkness of the cave, to be very bright.

"We should leave, Ma'am," Captain Gayozy said in a low voice.

"I think I have dropped something," Ilona an-swered. "Is it possible for you to find a light?"

"There is another lantern here," Captain Gayozy re-plied. "We brought a dozen with us, but the Prince thought we would only have need of half that num-ber."

"Please light one."

Ilona waited while Captain Gayozy carried out her request. Then as he brought the flickering candle-lan-tern back to her side she said:

"Perhaps you would carry it as we go along the passage."

"We cannot do that, Ma'am," Captain Gayozy said. "You heard His Highness's instructions."

"I have no intention of returning to the Castle," Ilona replied.

"But you cannot stay here, Ma'am. There will be fighting and you might be injured."

"I am not a fool, Captain Gayozy. I will not leave the passage at the other end until it is safe to do so. At the same time, I have no intention of leaving the Palace without the Prince."

She looked at the Captain and realised he was extremely disconcerted by her declaration.

He was a young officer, one of the Aides-de-Camp who had looked at her with admiration when he travelled opposite her in the carriage.

Now, despite his consternation, he could not stop his eyes from lingering for a moment on the red of her hair as it glittered in the candlelight.

"Do not be faint-hearted, Captain Gayozy," Ilona said with a touch of amusement in her voice. "You can hardly force me to return at the point of a pistol, and having brought the Prince safely here and found the secret passage, I have no intention of being sent home like an unwanted parcel!"

"I shall be court-martialled for dereliction of duty, Ma'am!" the Captain protested.

"Nonsense!" Ilona retorted. "You will be decorated for courage in the face of an extremely formidable enemy!"

The Captain could not help laughing.

"You are incorrigible, Ma'am. But I cannot allow you to take any risks."

"I will allow you to be very careful of my safety," Ilona promised him. "Now let us go up above and see what is happening!"

She remembered what a steep climb it was up the stone steps, and she had been right in assuring the Count that the passage, which had lasted for centuries, would not have changed in the last nine years.

It smelt dry and dusty and occasionally there were cobwebs that broke against Ilona's hair, but otherwise they had no difficulty in reaching the door that led into the Palace.

Here the Captain paused.

"We dare not go any further, Ma'am."

"What I suggest," Ilona replied, "is that you go and explore. Find out what is happening. Then, if it is safe, come back and collect me."

"I will leave the lantern with you, Ma'am."

"If we had had any sense we would have brought two with us," Ilona answered. "As it is, you must take it with you, otherwise you will never find the way. I will sit here in the darkness. I am not afraid."

"You are quite sure? I ought not to leave you."

"You must leave me," Ilona answered, "or else I shall have to stay here indefinitely, and if the Prince leaves the Palace by the front entrance, he might even forget about us."

"I am sure he would not do that!" the Captain answered.

Ilona knew that he must be aching to find out what was happening, and she realised that it had in fact been very frustrating for him not to be able to join his comrades in their enterprise.

"Go along, Captain," she said, "and try not to forget that I am waiting here for your return."

"I will certainly not do that, Ma'am."

He moved through the door, carrying the lantern in his hand, and Ilona sat down on the ground.

She saw the light flickering in the distance until it was little more than a will o' the wisp, then there was only darkness.

Of one thing she was certain—there had been no pitched battle!

Thick though the Palace walls were, and despite the fact that they had entered through a very different part of the building, she was sure that if there had been pistol- or rifle-shots, they would have heard them.

The guns that were to bombard Vitózi had certainly not been fired.

It seemed to Ilona, sitting in the darkness, that a century of time passed before she heard footsteps approaching on the stone floor and then saw the light of a lantern.

132

She was standing, waiting, when the Captain rejoined her.

"Everything is all right, Ma'am," he said.

She realised he was no longer speaking in a whisper but in quite a loud tone because he was excited.

"The Prince and our men took the Russians entirely by surprise! They were all asleep, Ma'am, if you can believe it, and only the sentries were on duty, looking out of the Palace in the other direction. They surrendered without a shot being fired!"

Ilona felt her fear, which had made every breath she drew an inescapable pain, subsiding.

"And the Prince?" she asked.

"He has gone with the rest of the troops to join our men at the pass. He has taken with him as prisoners the Russians who were captured in the Palace, but he intends not to keep them in Dabrozka, but to put them over the border into their own land."

"And . . . the King?" Ilona asked in a low voice.

"His Majesty has gone with them!"

Ilona gave a sigh of relief.

She had been afraid, although she had not admitted it to herself, of facing her father.

"Who is left in the Palace?" she asked.

"Only the servants, Ma'am. I have told them you are here, and they are preparing your room so that you can rest until the Prince returns."

"Thank you, Captain Gayozy."

He led Ilona through the cold, uninviting corridors until they reached the part of the Palace that was lived in.

Even then, there was a long walk to the State Apartments that she had used before her marriage.

When she reached them there were servants, hurriedly dressed, smiling a welcome.

Ilona paused in the Hall.

"I have a feeling, Captain Gayozy, that now that you have fulfilled your duty to me, you would wish to join His Majesty and your comrades."

She saw the delight in the young man's eyes.

"Do you think I could do that, Ma'am?"

"I am sure they will not be very far ahead, and you can catch them up," she answered. "I shall be quite safe in the Palace."

"You are adequately guarded, Ma'am. There are sentries on duty on the roof, on the battlements, and outside the front door!"

Ilona smiled.

"They certainly did not expect us to enter the way we did!"

"From all I have heard from the officers to whom I spoke, the Russians thought we must have dropped from the sky!"

Ilona laughed.

"Does the Prince know I am here?" she enquired.

Captain Gayozy looked a little embarrassed.

"He was very busy, Ma'am. I thought it best not to trouble him at the moment. They were just leaving when I learnt what had happened."

"You were quite right not to tell His Highness," Ilona said. "It would only worry him. When everything is quiet and peaceful, you can tell him I am here at the Palace. I shall sleep in my own bed. Goodnight, Captain."

The Captain drew himself up to attention and saluted.

"Good-night, Ma'am, and may I tell you how wonderful you have been?"

"Thank you, Captain," Ilona replied.

She went to her room, where the Housekeeper and two of the housemaids were waiting to attend to her.

As she undressed they chattered away excitedly, telling her how frightened they had been when the Russians arrived at the Palace and how unpleasant and rude the soldiers were!

"And greedy, Your Royal Highness! You wouldn't believe what they ate! If they'd stayed any longer we'd have been eaten out of house and home!"

"They will not trouble us again," Ilona said with a smile.

"But . . . His Majesty. . . ?" one of the maids murmured.

Ilona did not answer. The girl was asking the same question she had been asking herself.

What would the King do when he reached Russia? Would he incite them to make another effort to capture Dabrozka?

Would he invite them to invade the country, even without the excuse of restoring order in a civil war?

It was frightening to contemplate and suddenly Ilona felt very tired.

The Housekeeper had found her a night-gown, and as she got into bed the woman said:

"You will have a gown to wear tomorrow, Your Royal Highness. Quite a number of boxes have arrived from Paris containing garments that you must have ordered."

"Of course!" Ilona exclaimed. "I had arranged for them to be sent after me."

"His Majesty forbade us to have them conveyed to the Castle, Your Royal Highness," the Housekeeper explained. "But as I was sure you would not wish them to be creased, I hung them up in the wardrobe. They are there waiting for you."

"Thank you," Ilona said sleepily.

She was so tired that her eye-lids were dropping even as she spoke.

It had been a long ride, and so much else had happened during the day, which had all been exhausting.

First she had been kidnapped by the *Zyghes*, then there was her rescue by the Prince when he had lifted her bodily from the saddle, and the fear she had felt when she learnt that the Russians were actually in the Palace, intending to bombard Vitózi!

It all had taken its toll of her strength!

When she was alone she remembered too the passionate emotions she had felt the previous evening, and the jealousy that had kept her tossing and turning all night and prevented her from sleeping.

"I will not think about the gypsy," she told herself.

Deliberately she sent her thoughts back to the moment when the Prince had held her in his arms and

135

she had heard his heart beating as her cheek lay against his shoulder.

She tried to imagine that she was still with him and could feel again that sense of safety and protection because he was close.

"I love . . . him! I love him with my . . . heart and . . . soul," Ilona whispered.

She fell asleep pretending that once again she was in his arms.

Chapter Seven

Ilona awoke because someone was pulling back the curtains.

She felt drowsy with sleep, then suddenly she remembered where she was and what had brought her there.

She sat up in bed and saw that the Housekeeper was bringing in a tray to set down beside her.

"What time is it?" she asked.

"It is well after noon, Your Royal Highness, but I let you sleep on, seeing how tired you were."

"As late as that?" Ilona exclaimed. "Then what has happened?"

"Most of the troops have returned. They are celebrating a victory!"

"There was fighting?"

"Very little, I think, Your Royal Highness. His Highness is safe. He came back some hours ago. He had a short rest, and now I believe he is outside the Palace with the troops."

Ilona was silent for a moment. Then she asked in a very low voice:

"Did . . . His Highness enquire . . . after me?"

"No, Your Royal Highness."

There seemed to be nothing more to say, and Ilona without tasting it ate some of the food that had been brought to her. Then, having had a bath, she started to dress.

She thought as she did so that it was typical of her relationship with her husband that now, when she was of no further use to him, he had no interest in her.

Last night he had spoken to her as if she was a

human being instead of someone he hated, and she had thought when he had taken her hand to lead her as they walked towards the Palace that he was no longer as cold as he had been ever since they were married.

But now it seemed that she had been mistaken.

Now that all the excitement was over, their relationship was back on its previous unhappy footing.

Ilona felt so depressed that she let the Housekeeper dress her in one of her new gowns that had come from Paris, without even noticing what she wore.

It was pale blue trimmed with white lace, and she vaguely remembered buying it but felt no particular interest in it.

When she was ready she left her bed-room and walked along the corridor that led to the top of the stairs.

Down in the Great Hall there were officers in small groups talking to one another, and she could see through the open door and the tall windows that there were troops outside in the court-yard.

Then as she looked at them, expecting to see the Prince, she suddenly stiffened.

Coming up the drive towards the Palace was a bunch of colourful gypsies.

There was no mistaking the full skirts of the women, the red coat of the *Voivode*, and the other gypsies with their bright sashes and silk handkerchiefs tied over their dark heads.

With an exclamation beneath her breath, Ilona turned away, feeling the same stabbing pain in her heart that she had endured the night the Prince had danced with Mautya.

The gypsy dancer had certainly wasted no time in crossing the river and following the Prince.

'Perhaps he sent a message for her to join him,' Ilona thought to herself.

He needed his mistress in his hour of triumph but not the company of his wife.

She walked down the corridor not thinking where she was going, only wanting to be rid of the sight of the gypsies.

She could see all too vividly the beautiful face of the dancer with her enticing dark slanting eyes and her red, inviting mouth.

Then Ilona decided to visit the rooms that Julius had occupied, thinking, as she had thought last night, that it was actually her brother who had been instrumental in saving Dabrozka from the Russians.

If Julius had not determined to creep out at night against the King's wishes, and if she had not been his accomplice, then at this very moment the Russian shells would be bursting over Vitózi.

She thought how much Julius would have enjoyed the excitement of taking the Russians unawares, but it was the Prince who had carried out the whole operation so brilliantly that there had been no blood-shed.

She stopped in the corridor, realising that she had reached not Julius's room but the Nursery that she had occupied until the day she had left the Castle with her mother eight years ago.

She opened the door and found that it was exactly as she had left it.

There was the big arm-chair by the tiled stove where she had sat with her mother and listened to fairy-stories, which had entranced her.

There was her rocking-horse, which she had loved passionately until when she was four years old she had been allowed to ride a pony, and found it an enchantment that had made all her other toys fade into insignificance.

But she had never thrown them away and there was still the dolls'-house that had been made especially for her by the citizens of Vitózi, to resemble the Palace in miniature.

And there was the fort that they had presented to Julius when he was a small boy.

Both models were exquisitely carved and decorated by Dabrozkan craftsmen with their inimitable skill.

Iolna walked across the room to touch the dolls'-house.

Standing near it she saw the painted cupboard in which she had been made to tidy away her smaller toys before she was taken to bed.

She opened the door of the cupboard and saw lying on one of the shelves the first doll she had ever owned, which she had loved more than all the others.

It had fair hair and blue eyes and her mother had spent many hours stitching beautiful lace-trimmed clothes in which Ilona dressed and undressed her favourite.

She picked it up, then made an exclamation of distress, for the face was smashed!

There was a great crack across the small pink-and-white nose and a piece of porcelain was missing from one rosy cheek.

Ilona stared down at it, and somehow finding that her doll was broken was the final straw in the misery that had been accumulating in her ever since she awoke.

It was as if the broken face told her all too clearly that her own life was broken while the beauty of it was destroyed.

She held the doll for a moment in her hands, then enfolding it against her breast she began to cry.

At first the tears ran down her cheeks slowly like the snows in the mountains beginning to melt, then they became a tempest!

All the misery, unhappiness, and loneliness she had felt ever since her wedding-day seemed to flood over her in an agony that was unbearable.

She sank down onto the floor, and still cuddling the doll in her arms bent her head and wept so that her whole body shook.

She did not hear the door open until suddenly a voice said:

"I have been looking for you. . . ."

Ilona did not raise her head.

She was past caring who saw her. She had no pride left. It had collapsed to the point where she was oblivious of everything but her own despair.

"What has happened? Why are you crying?" the Prince asked.

Then as Ilona did not answer he said insistently:

"What has upset you? I never imagined you could cry like this!"

She heard his voice and somehow knew that she must answer him.

"I . . . c-cannot . . . help it," she sobbed. "I am so . . . alone . . . so miserable. . . . Y-you hate me and I want to . . . die!"

"Hate you?" the Prince repeated in a strange voice.

Then he bent down and pulled her to her feet.

Ilona reacted automatically to the pressure of his hands.

She could hardly realise he was there. She was too encompassed with the dark cloud of her own unhappiness to realise fully what was happening.

"Y-you . . . have everything!" she sobbed. "The p-people love you and you have the . . . gypsy . . . she has come . . . here to you . . . but I am . . . alone . . . unwanted . . . I have not . . . even a . . . baby to love."

"My absurd, foolish little Princess," the Prince said in his deep voice.

Then he picked her up and sat down in the arm-chair, cradling her in his arms.

Ilona felt a tremor run through her because she was close to him, but she could not control the torrent of her tears and she went on crying against his shoulder.

"It has all been a dreadful misunderstanding," the Prince said quietly. "Stop crying, my darling, and I will try to explain what has happened."

Ilona raised her face. The tears were running down her cheeks, but her eyes looked up into his.

"W-what . . . did you . . . call me?" she whispered.

"I called you my darling," he answered, "which you have been since the first moment I saw you."

"It is . . . not true!"

He pulled her closer to him and kissed first her wet eyes, then the tears on her cheeks, and lastly her mouth.

As Ilona felt his lips again and the hard possessive pressure of them, which she had never forgotten, she felt as if a streak of lightning shot through her body.

The fire that had burnt so fiercely within her when she had watched him dancing with the gypsy rose now in a thousand flickering flames, burning through her from the very tips of her toes to her lips, which he held captive.

This was what she had longed for, what she had known she would feel if he kissed her again, what she had missed, and what she thought she would never know.

He kissed her fiercely, possessively, and yet at the same time there was a tenderness that she could not describe, although she knew it was there.

When finally he raised his head to look down at her, her eyes were shining like stars, and her mouth was very soft and trembling.

"I . . . thought you . . . hated me," she said, and her voice was a little hoarse, although there was an irrepressible lilt in it.

"I love you!"

"B-but you were . . . so cold . . . so cruel," she whispered. "You came to my room and you never even . . . looked at me!"

The Prince drew her a little closer.

"If I had allowed myself to do so, I could never have refrained from kissing you and making you mine; but I thought that your father was speaking for you when he said that you loathed me."

"How could . . . you have . . . thought that?"

"You carried yourself so stiffly when we were married and when we drove back to the Palace," he said. "How was I to know that it was because that devil had beaten you?"

Ilona's eyes fell before his.

"Who . . . could have told . . . you that?"

"Does it matter?" the Prince asked. "I deeply regret, my precious one, that we should from the very beginning have had secrets from each other."

"I thought you . . . despised me when you first . . . kissed me," Ilona murmured.

"I thought you were the most beautiful person I had ever seen," the Prince answered. "But when you did not respond to my kiss, I thought you were as cold and indifferent as you said you were."

Ilona did not answer and he turned her face up to his to say:

"It was not until yesterday that I understood, and realised that you were only very inexperienced."

Now there was no mistaking the flood of colour in Ilona's cheeks and the Prince asked gently:

"How many men have kissed you, my sweet?"

"Only . . . you."

He made a sound as if of triumph, and then his lips were on hers and the walls whirled round them as she clung to him with a sudden passion that she could not repress.

"Then I am the first and the last!" the Prince said, and his voice was unsteady. "I am so jealous, my darling, that I will want to kill any man who so much as looks at you!"

"You are . . . jealous?" Ilona asked quickly. "But I . . ."

Her voice died away.

"I would like you to finish that sentence," the Prince said.

She hid her face against him.

"I was . . . so jealous when you . . . danced with the gypsy, I . . . I was sure she was your . . . m-mistress!"

"I wanted you to be jealous," the Prince said. "That was the reason why I took you to the gypsy party—I wished to see if the music would arouse you."

He laughed very gently as he said:

"I had really begun to believe that you had only ice in your veins!"

Ilona remembered the murderous feelings she had felt for Mautya.

"I loved you so . . . much," she murmured, "that I wanted to . . . kill the . . . dancer!"

"I wish I had known."

"You never . . . came to me that . . . night."

"I did not trust myself," he answered. "But Mautya is not my mistress, my precious one. She is in fact very happily married to the *Voivode*, who would undoubtedly stab me to death if I should even approach his wife in such a manner!"

"Oh . . . I am . . . glad, so very, very glad!" Ilona whispered. "I could not sleep for thinking of you."

"And I could not sleep for wanting you, my dearest

heart," the Prince said. "But I thought when I saw you leaving the gypsy gathering that you were merely shocked, and that my efforts to make your heart beat faster and bring a flicker of fire into your eyes had failed."

"If only I had . . . known you . . . felt like . . . that."

"How could you look so proud, so unemotional, and at the same time so exquisitely beautiful?" the Prince asked.

"Mama taught me always to control my feelings," Ilona said simply.

"That is something you must never do again, my lovely one, not where I am concerned," the Prince answered.

He was kissing her again, his lips moving over the softness of her skin.

He kissed the white column of her neck, arousing the fire that burnt within her until her breath came quickly between her lips and she stirred in his arms.

"My precious! Heart of my heart! My dream come true! I have so much to teach you!" the Prince murmured, and his teeth touched the lobes of her small ears.

He felt the quiver that ran through her.

"Do I excite you?" he asked.

"You . . . know you . . . do!"

"What do you feel? Tell me!"

She hid her face against his neck.

"Wild . . . very, very wild . . ."

"What else?"

"There are little . . . flames flickering . . . inside me."

"I will make them leap higher and higher and become a blaze!"

His hands were caressing her and her lips sought his.

"You do . . . really love me?"

It was the question of a child who wants to be reassured.

"I love you until it is impossible to think of anything else," the Prince replied. "You do not know how you have tortured me and what an unspeakable hell it was to sit in your bed-room night after night, seeing your wonderful hair falling over your shoulders and knowing I dare not come near you."

"You never . . . looked at . . . me," Ilona said accusingly.

"I saw you," the Prince said. "I saw you with my heart, and with my soul. I knew that you belonged to me, but your father had erected that impassable barrier between us and I would not humiliate myself by attempting to break it down."

"I . . . wanted you . . . too. I wanted you . . . unbearably!" Ilona whispered.

"There are no barriers now," the Prince said, "and there will never be any in the future. I will love you, look after you, and worship you for the rest of my life!"

"That is all I want," Ilona said with a deep sigh. "I only feel safe when I am in your arms . . . like yesterday when you . . . saved me from the *Zyghes*."

"It was difficult not to kiss you then, when you were so close to me," the Prince said, "and I will never be able to tell you what I suffered when I thought those savage brutes would hide you where I would never be able to find you."

"I think . . . Papa paid them to . . . kidnap me," Ilona said in a low voice.

"That is true," the Prince replied. "The men we took prisoner confessed that they had been given a large sum of money to take you away to their caves in the mountains."

He drew a deep breath.

"It was just chance that I chose to ride back through the woods after my meeting was over and encountered the groom who had accompanied you!"

"How could Papa be so . . . cruel to me?" Ilona murmured, and then asked apprehensively, "Where is he now?"

"We drove the Russian troops across the border," the Prince answered, "and he was with them."

"They will not . . . return?"

"I think it unlikely they will attempt it. Our troops

are guarding the pass, and from now on Dabrozka is going to be a united land, so there will be no excuse for foreign intervention."

He kissed Ilona again before he said:

"That reminds me, my sweet, the reason that I came to find you was that the Prime Minister and members of the Council wish to speak to you."

"You did not . . . ask to see me . . . this morning!" Ilona said wistfully.

"I did not know you were in the Palace," the Prince replied. "Gayozy told me where you were only a few minutes ago. I had expected my orders to be obeyed and believed that you were safely at the Castle."

There was a smile on his lips as he said:

"Had you forgotten that in the marriage-service you promised to obey me?"

"I wanted to be . . . near you."

"That is a perfect excuse, and one I am only too willing to accept!"

He kissed her gently as if she was infinitely precious, before he said:

"We must go downstairs, my adorable one. There will be plenty of time, when everyone has gone, for us to talk about ourselves and for you to tell me that you really do not hate me."

"I love you! I love you more than I can ever . . . begin to put into . . . words!" Ilona said passionately.

"If you say things like that," the Prince answered with a sudden deep note in his voice, "the Prime Minister will have to wait!"

"We must . . . do our . . . duty."

The Prince rose from the arm-chair and pulled Ilona to her feet, then he put his arms round her and held her so close that it was hard to breathe.

"You are mine!" he said fiercely. "Every perfect little piece of you. I am jealous of the very air you breathe!"

She felt herself thrill at the desire in his voice. Then as resolutely, with what was obviously an effort, he turned towards the door, she said:

"I cannot go . . . down like . . . this! I must bathe my . . . eyes."

"You look very beautiful just as you are," the Prince replied.

They walked hand in hand down the corridor and when Ilona went into her bed-room he followed her.

She bathed her eyes in cold water, then the Prince dried her face with a soft towel before he kissed her lips, her eyes, and once again her neck.

"I want to take the pins out of your hair," he said, "and see it fall over your shoulders."

"You have . . . seen it like . . . that."

Her voice was quivering because he was so close, and because his kisses had evoked such incredible sensations that her whole body vibrated with them.

"I have seen it, but I have not touched it," he answered. "And never, my bewitching little wife—do you understand?—never are you to allow any other man to see you as you looked yesterday evening when you came into the Hunting-Room!"

There was a masterful note in his voice, which thrilled her.

"I thought as you were not . . . interested in me," she said, "that it would not matter how I . . . appeared."

"And now that you know I am *interested*," he said, accentuating the word, "you will behave very much more circumspectly!"

Ilona laughed from sheer happiness.

"I thought you . . . wanted me to be . . . wild and . . . unrestrained."

"That is what you will be, but only with me," the Prince answered. "To everyone else you must continue to be proud and cold, a snow-Princess with ice in her veins!"

"I think it will be . . . impossible for me . . . ever to feel like . . . that again," she whispered.

And as her lips sought his she saw the smouldering fire in his eyes and a flame united them. . . .

* * *

Ilona tidied her hair, then with her eyes filled with sunshine and her face radiant with happiness they walked down the stairs together.

Only as they reached the door into the Throne-

Room, where Ilona had last been after her wedding, did she wonder vaguely what the Prime Minister had to say to her.

But there was no time to think and she entered the Hall of Mirrors to find it half-filled with Statesmen she had met before and who all held positions of importance in the Government.

The Prime Minister raised her hand to his lips. Then as Ilona waited he said:

"We came here this afternoon, Your Royal Highness, as representatives of the Government of Dabrozka, in His Majesty's absence, to discuss the position of the Monarchy. But in the last few minutes we have received a communication that completely alters what we came to say."

"A communication?" Ilona enquired, but the Prime Minister was speaking to the Prince.

"The officer was in fact, Your Highness, looking for you," the Prime Minister said. "He came from the troops you left guarding the Eastern border."

"What has happened?" the Prince asked quickly.

"It is with deep regret that I have to inform Her Royal Highness," the Prime Minister said slowly, "that His Majesty the King is dead!"

Ilona put her hand into the Prince's.

She felt as if she wanted to hold on to him, not because she was upset but simply because the relief of it made her feel dizzy.

She had known, even though the King had left Dabrozka, that he would still menace the peace of the country.

"How did His Majesty die?" the Prince asked.

"The officer commanding your troops, Your Highness, was told by the Russians that His Majesty was upset by his treatment when he reached Russian soil. Apparently in a rage he killed three Russian officers and the others were forced to protect themselves."

The Prime Minister looked again at Ilona.

"On behalf of myself and my colleagues, Your Royal Highness, we can only offer you our deepest condolences."

"Thank you," Ilona said gravely.

There was a moment's silence. Then the Prime Minister said in a very different tone of voice:

"But Your Royal Highness will understand that the Government of the country must continue. We therefore offer you not the Regency of Dabrozka, as we had intended in the King's absence, but the Crown!"

Ilona was still holding tightly to the Prince's hand, then in a low voice that was however quite steady she said:

"I am deeply honoured that you should wish me to become Queen of this lovely land, but I consider the difficulties that lie ahead and the problems that have to be solved in the near future are beyond the powers of a woman."

She saw the surprise in the Prime Minister's eyes as she continued:

"I therefore wish to refuse the position you offer me, but suggest, if you will allow me to do so, that as the Radák line ends with me, it is time there was a Sáros on the Throne!"

There was an audible sound that she thought was one of approval from the representatives who had been listening attentively and in complete silence to what she said.

"I want to serve Dabrozka and its people," Ilona went on. "I want my country to find peace and prosperity, and I can imagine no-one better fitted to achieve these aims than my husband, Prince Aladár!"

She looked up at the Prince as she spoke and felt his fingers tighten on hers.

"The only position I want to occupy," she continued softly, "is that of his wife!"

The Prince looked into her eyes and the cheers that rang out seemed to vibrate against the mirrors and echo and re-echo round the Throne-Room.

"I know I am speaking for everyone present," the Prime Minister said, "when I say that we will accept Your Royal Highness's recommendation whole-heartedly and without reserve!"

His voice rang out as he went on:

"Prince Aladár Sáros, will you accept the Throne of

Dabrozka and become the first Sáros to reign over our country?"

"I will!"

The Prince's voice was very grave, and yet there was a positiveness about it that made Ilona's heart leap.

"The King is dead—long live the King!"

As the Prime Minister went down on one knee he was followed by every man present.

Holding Ilona by the hand, the Prince drew her onto the dais and she sat down on the Queen's Throne.

Then as the Prime Minister rose to his feet the Prince seated himself and they all moved forward to pay him homage.

* * *

It was very much later that evening that Ilona and Aladár walked up the Grand Staircase.

She was wearing one of the beautiful gowns that had come from Paris.

Of green tulle caught at the sides with water-lilies, it made Ilona's eyes very green, and accentuated the brilliance of her hair.

They had been cheered by the soldiers outside the Palace and Ilona had seen for the first time the Radák and the Sáros Regiments on parade together.

It was when they had finished inspecting the Guard of Honour that Ilona had noticed that the gypsies were encamped outside the Palace gates.

As they walked away from the parade the Prince had said in a low voice that only she could hear:

"I forgot to tell you that I was unjustly accused."

"By whom?" she asked in surprise.

"By you!"

She looked at him enquiringly and he explained:

"The gypsies who you thought had followed me here had actually come to petition you!"

"Me?" Ilona exclaimed in amazement.

"As the King was no longer in the country, they believed that you had the power to rescind the laws that prohibited them from being on Radák land."

"How could I guess that was the . . . reason for their coming to the Palace so quickly?"

"I shall have to teach you to trust me, my suspicious darling, amongst other things!"

There was a look in his eyes that made her thrill, but then there was no more time for intimate conversation.

There was a dinner-party at which the Chef had done marvels considering that at short notice he had had to provide a meal for fifty guests.

Fortunately they did not stay long, and left talking of meetings that had to take place the following day and the preparations that were to be put into operation immediately for the Coronation.

"You will be the most handsome King Dabrozka has ever known," Ilona said to her husband as they reached the top of the stairs.

"And it would be impossible to find a more beautiful Queen in the whole world," he replied.

She gave a little sigh of sheer happiness. Then as they entered the bed-room she found to her surprise that there were no maids waiting for her.

Aladár came into the room and shut the door behind him.

"I told them not to stay up for you," he said, as if anticipating the question Ilona had not asked.

He saw the light that came into her eyes and as he walked towards her he said:

"I could not wait any longer to have you to myself."

He pulled her almost roughly against him, and as his lips came down crushingly on hers, his fingers pulled the pins from her hair.

A great cloud of red-gold tresses fell over her white shoulders and he kissed a handful of it before once again he kissed her lips.

"You are mine!" he said. "Mine, completely and absolutely! Tonight I am going to undress you as I have wanted to do ever since we were married!"

"You are . . . making me . . . shy," Ilona whispered.

"I love you when you are shy," he answered, "but not when you are proud."

"I will never be proud again," she answered, "except

151

that I am very proud to be your wife and . . . overwhelmingly proud because you . . . love me!"

She was not able to say any more.

Aladár was kissing her with a passion that made the flames of desire rise higher and higher within them both.

It was all-consuming and their need for each other made Ilona feel as if they leapt into the fire itself and it was impossible to think or feel, but only to burn.

She felt Aladár's fingers undoing her gown, and as it fell to the floor he lifted her in his arms.

With his mouth holding her captive, he carried her away into a glorious secret kingdom of their own where there was no pride . . . only a fiery, uncontrolled, ecstatic love.

ABOUT THE AUTHOR

BARBARA CARTLAND, the celebrated romantic author, historian, playwright, lecturer, political speaker and television personality, has now written over 150 books. Miss Cartland has had a number of historical books published and several biographical ones, including that of her brother, Major Ronald Cartland, who was the first Member of Parliament to be killed in the War. This book had a Foreword by Sir Winston Churchill.

In private life, Barbara Cartland, who is a Dame of the Order of St. John of Jerusalem, has fought for better conditions and salaries for Midwives and nurses. As President of the Royal College of Midwives (Hertfordshire Branch), she has been invested with the first Badge of Office ever given in Great Britain, which was subscribed to by the Midwives themselves. She has also championed the cause for old people and founded the first Romany Gypsy Camp in the world.

Barbara Cartland is deeply interested in Vitamin Therapy and is President of the British National Association for Health.

Barbara Cartland

The world's bestselling author of romantic fiction. Her stories are always captivating tales of intrigue, adventure and love.

☐	THE TEARS OF LOVE	2148	$1.25
☐	THE DEVIL IN LOVE	2149	$1.25
☐	THE ELUSIVE EARL	2436	$1.25
☐	THE BORED BRIDEGROOM	6381	$1.25
☐	JOURNEY TO PARADISE	6383	$1.25
☐	THE PENNILESS PEER	6387	$1.25
☐	NO DARKNESS FOR LOVE	6427	$1.25
☐	THE LITTLE ADVENTURE	6428	$1.25
☐	LESSONS IN LOVE	6431	$1.25
☐	THE DARING DECEPTION	6435	$1.25
☐	CASTLE OF FEAR	8103	$1.25
☐	THE GLITTERING LIGHTS	8104	$1.25
☐	A SWORD TO THE HEART	8105	$1.25
☐	THE MAGNIFICENT MARRIAGE	8166	$1.25
☐	THE RUTHLESS RAKE	8240	$1.25
☐	THE DANGEROUS DANDY	8280	$1.25
☐	THE WICKED MARQUIS	8467	$1.25
☐	LOVE IS INNOCENT	8505	$1.25
☐	THE FRIGHTENED BRIDE	8780	$1.25
☐	THE FLAME IS LOVE	8887	$1.25

Barbara Cartland

The world's bestselling author of romantic fiction.
Her stories are always captivating tales of intrigue,
adventure and love.

☐	A VERY NAUGHTY ANGEL	2107	$1.25
☐	THE CRUEL COUNT	2128	$1.25
☐	CALL OF THE HEART	2140	$1.25
☐	AS EAGLES FLY	2147	$1.25
☐	THE MASK OF LOVE	2366	$1.25
☐	AN ARROW OF LOVE	2426	$1.25
☐	A GAMBLE WITH HEARTS	2430	$1.25
☐	A KISS FOR THE KING	2433	$1.25
☐	A FRAME OF DREAMS	2434	$1.25
☐	THE FRAGRANT FLOWER	2435	$1.25
☐	MOON OVER EDEN	2437	$1.25
☐	THE GOLDEN ILLUSION	2449	$1.25
☐	FIRE ON THE SNOW	2450	$1.25
☐	THE HUSBAND HUNTERS	2461	$1.25
☐	THE SHADOW OF SIN	6430	$1.25
☐	SAY YES, SAMANTHA	7834	$1.25
☐	THE KARMA OF LOVE	8106	$1.25
☐	BEWITCHED	8630	$1.25
☐	THE IMPETUOUS DUCHESS	8705	$1.25

Buy them at your local bookseller or use this handy coupon:

Bantam Book Catalog

It lists over a thousand money-saving best-sellers originally priced from $3.75 to $15.00 —bestsellers that are yours now for as little as 60¢ to $2.95!

The catalog gives you a great opportunity to build your own private library at huge savings!

So don't delay any longer—send us your name and address and 25¢ (to help defray postage and handling costs).